Hidden Secrets

Hidden Secrets

Carolyn Brown

Montlake Romance

Text copyright © 2012 Carolyn Brown
All rights reserved.
Printed in the United States of America.

Published by Montlake Romance
P.O. Box 400818
Las Vegas, NV 89140

ISBN-13: 9781612186610
ISBN-10: 1612186610

To Pam Lovett
Remembering all the good times!

CHAPTER ONE

A grown man of twenty-five didn't cry because his overbearing, overopinionated, and bossy old neighbor died. Not even if she had been his surrogate grandmother and good friend all rolled into one. But Luke O'Neal let the tears flood his blue eyes and drip onto his chambray work shirt without even one attempt to wipe them away. A warm spring breeze set Norma's rocking chair in motion—and set loose even more tears.

Three rocking chairs were lined up on the porch. The middle one belonged to Norma always. No one ever sat in it. The one on the end next to the mimosa tree was John's, and the remaining one belonged to Luke. That's where they shared their joys and sorrows at the end of several days a week. And now the middle one was empty, never to be filled again.

John Rayford rounded the end of the porch and sat down in the third rocking chair, leaving the one in the middle empty. He ran his fingers through his dark hair, which was sprinkled with bits of gray, especially in the temples. His green eyes were misty and his square jaw set in determination not to cry.

"I'll miss her. Seems like she ought to come on out of the house and sit with us."

Luke swallowed the lump in his throat and nodded.

"She was a pistol," John said.

Luke nodded again.

"You get the donkeys fed and Buster's leg taken care of?"

"Yes," he managed to get out one word.

"I called the cousins."

"Are they even coming out here? Never knew them to come in all the years I've been alive. And Norma talked about them all the time, like she just saw them last week."

John nodded. "They'll be here in four days. And then they can take over."

"Reckon they'll know jack squat about farmin'?"

"Guess they can learn if they don't take one look and take off like a scalded hound back to their hotel and wineries."

"I'm not going to like them."

"Norma didn't say we had to like them. She said we had to help them if they needed it."

"Well, I'm not going to. I wouldn't be surprised if Buster and Sparky both lay down and die in the next couple of weeks without her. Dogs do that, you know, so donkeys might too."

Seconds ticked off the clock so slowly that Kim wondered if time stood still. Minutes lasted three days past eternity. Finally the time passed. She pushed her long, straight dishwater-blonde hair behind her ears and shut her blue eyes as she picked the plastic stick from the cup beside the bathroom sink. Dizziness drove her to sit on the vanity stool, but she still didn't open her eyes. When she did, she was glad she was sitting down.

"Pregnant," she whispered.

Four generations of Brewer women who had been born with haloes and wings, and she had to be the one who brought disgrace upon the whole family. Granted, her grandfather was a 100-percent-guaranteed, bona fide rascal, but he wasn't one of the Brewer women. They were beyond reproach, bordering on modern-day saints. Perhaps she'd inherited more of her genes from her rogue grandfather, Daniel Tarleton, rather than her flawless great-grandmother, Hannah Brewer; her grandmother, Karen Tarleton; or her mother, Sue DeHaven.

She tossed the stick in the trash can and touched her flat stomach. A baby grew in there. One she and Marshall Neville made six weeks before, the only night they were married.

Talk about unlucky—that was Kim DeHaven! What was she going to do with a baby? Her great-grandmother would fire her; her grandmother, crucify her; her mother would sell her into slavery.

Not really, but they'd sure enough feel like it. How on earth did this happen? It was just one time, for heaven's sake!

She groaned. She couldn't even tell Marshall, not when he'd just asked his girlfriend to marry him in a real wedding come Christmastime. What a tangled-up mess—and she had no idea how to unravel it.

She'd met Marshall two months ago. His cousin was getting married, and the wedding party stayed at the Brewer Hotel. He'd come out to visit with them. After multiple calls and lots of texting, he'd asked her out, and that led to going with him on spring break to Las Vegas. It started out as a crazy dare and by the next morning, they realized just how foolish they had been when they woke up married. When they got home that evening, Marshall's father had taken them straight to his lawyer and it had been annulled.

A month later, she'd gotten a text from Marshall saying that he and Amelia, his girlfriend since high school, were back together and planning a Christmas wedding.

She wandered aimlessly into the bedroom of the two-room suite she occupied on the ground floor of the lavish Brewer Hotel in Morgantown, West Virginia. When she graduated high school two years before, Hannah had presented her a key to her own suite. She had a king-size bed, an entertainment unit with cable television and stereo, her own laptop with Wi-Fi, a huge closet, a living room with a comfortable deep sofa and recliner, and a small apartment-sized refrigerator with a microwave on top tucked into a corner for snacks.

She'd worked at the hotel in some capacity since she'd turned sixteen. She helped at the front desk and with the bookings, generally keeping an eye on things in the evenings. But mostly in the summer, she was at her great-grandmother's beck and call to do whatever she wanted.

Hannah Brewer and her late husband, Jesse, had owned it since the day they married, more than sixty years before. To stay at the Brewer was an experience, instead of a mere place to throw the suitcases and splash in a swimming pool. The only reason it was a five-star hotel was because they didn't give out six or seven or ten stars.

Hannah and Jesse had only one child—a daughter, Karen, who married Daniel Tarleton. Karen was even more perfect than Hannah was, if that was possible. Instead of a woman entering a room, a force strolled in when Karen arrived. She lived in the old Cosby plantation mansion outside of town, and the only fault she had was her judgment in men.

Or *man*, as in her husband of more than forty years. Good-looking beyond words with his salt-and-pepper hair and big brown eyes. Rumor had it if all the women he'd cheated on Karen with were put shoulder to shoulder, the line would reach from Morgantown to DC.

Sue DeHaven, Kim's mother, was a quiet schoolteacher. Her husband—Kim's father, Jeff—had died two years before in a tragic automobile accident. If Sue had a fault, Kim didn't know where she hid it. She'd been the perfect mother, and she was the one Kim hated to face the most.

Throwing herself down on the bed, she stared at the ceiling.

Show me what to do. Give me a sign. I can't face Nanna or Grandmother or even Momma.

The phone rang.

She jumped and grabbed it from her nightstand. The phone call could be her sign!

"Hello, Nanna." Did her voice sound different now that she was going to be a mother?

"How quick can you get up to my apartment?"

"Are you OK?" Kim asked.

"I'm fine, but hurry up…please," Hannah said.

Kim shivered at the tone of her great-grandmother's voice. Surely she hadn't figured out Kim's secret already.

"I'm on my way." Kim removed her nightshirt with Tweety Bird on the front and slipped into a pair of khaki shorts, an

5

orange T-shirt, and a pair of matching flip-flops, and then went straight to the elevator in the lobby.

When it stopped she knocked on Hannah's penthouse door.

Hannah started talking the minute she swung the door open. "I just got word that my cousin in Emet, Oklahoma, died this morning and left me her farm. I've decided to go out there and finish bringing in the summer crops."

Kim stepped through the door and looked around the room. Everything looked the same as it had the night before when she kissed her great-grandmother on the cheek and left.

"Where in the devil is Emet? You never mentioned a cousin or any relatives living in Oklahoma, or any relatives of any kind, period."

Hannah picked up the phone from an end table, but she didn't hit any buttons.

"We'll talk about that later. I need to call Sue and Karen. They don't know it, but they are going too."

"You want me to book flights for this afternoon?" Kim asked.

"I'm not flying. I'm riding and you're driving."

Kim wiggled her head. Surely she hadn't heard her grand-mother right. Oklahoma was a long way off and driving would take days. She couldn't begin to fathom driving that many days, much less with a fidgety, nearly eighty-year-old woman in the car.

"How big is this town? And what kind of ranch is it?" Kim asked.

"Just over a hundred, and it's a farm, not a ranch. Small orchard, big garden. Little fruit stand out by the road to sell the produce," Hannah said.

"Dear Lord!" Kim shuddered.

"God is dear, I'm sure, but even God can't keep me from going now that I've set my mind to it," Hannah said.

Her tall, elegant great-grandmother on a farm in Oklahoma was a vision Kim couldn't even drag up from the bottom of her imagination. Hannah Brewer, the queen of the Brewer Hotel, out in the middle of a garden? Hannah had never even been to the vineyards of the winery because she might break a perfectly manicured fingernail or a West Virginia breeze might ruffle her gray hair.

Hannah went on. "My mind is made up. Has been since John called this morning and told me Norma was dead. Didn't expect her to leave me the farm, but I'm not surprised. Anyway, I'm going and you are coming with me. Computers scare the dickens out of me, and John says everything she did was kept on one. He can't operate the stupid thing. You are good with them, so that is your new summer job."

"Nanna, who is John?"

"John Rayford, and he's Norma's neighbor on the north. Luke O'Neal is her neighbor on the south. They are both cattle ranchers and her place is a little hundred-and-twenty-acre stretch right between them. They were her friends and John called me this morning to tell me that she died about daybreak. She left him a letter telling him what to do. First thing was to tell me I inherited the farm. Next was to cremate her. The third was not to have a funeral," Hannah said.

"And why haven't you mentioned this woman? Does Momma or Grandmother know about her?" Kim asked.

"No, they don't. I'll explain it on the trip. You go on and call the rental place for a car or a van, and pack. Casual things, with maybe two outfits for church. We'll be attending the church in Milburn where she went."

Kim took a deep breath. "Nanna, you can't work in a garden or gather fruit."

"I can do anything I please, and don't you be telling me I can't." Hannah waved her away as she poked in her daughter's phone number with the other.

CHAPTER TWO

Karen Tarleton picked up a pen and held it over the divorce papers. She'd endured forty years of infidelity. Pretended she didn't know about Daniel's affairs, even when it was absolute, unadulterated gospel instead of malicious rumors. And now he had the nerve to sue her for divorce and half the assets. He wanted the winery *and* his twenty-five-year-old bimbo. Well, he wasn't going to get his way this time.

The only thing that had kept her sane all these years was making wine and marketing it. Daniel was not taking her half of the winery, not even if Tiffany—what kind of name was that anyway? It sounded like a place to buy jewelry, not a name. Too danged bad if his new child bride wanted the ex-wife completely out of the picture.

She laid the pen down and paced the floor, her long sheer robe swishing when she turned at the ends of the enormous bedroom. They'd worked fine together in the grapes from day one. She hadn't found out until after Sue was born that Daniel was an unfaithful rascal.

By then she had a daughter to raise, a name to protect. Her mother, Hannah, would have never forgiven her if she'd left Daniel. Hannah had never committed a sin in her entire life. She was the only daughter of Mary and Raymond Cosby of Morgantown, West Virginia, and society didn't run much higher than that. When she married Jesse Brewer, her father gave them the hotel business and retired to his vineyard. Just before Grandpa Cosby died, he gave the vineyard to Karen and Daniel.

Now Daniel wanted to buy out her half. She couldn't sign the papers. Karen wouldn't give up what she'd worked at for her whole life. She wouldn't disappoint her grandfather or her father, Jesse, by taking the easy way out.

Not this time.

She picked up her cell phone and dialed the lawyer's number.

"This is Karen Tarleton. I need to speak to Dale," she said and waited. "Good morning, Dale. I have the divorce papers right here. I won't sell Daniel my half. I know he's entitled to his portion and the law will uphold that. We've worked this winery together for forty years. He's going to have to continue to be partners with me or sell me his half. If the new wife doesn't want him around me, that's her problem."

Karen pushed the end button before the lawyer tried to talk her out of her decision. The phone rang before she even had time to put it back on her bedside table.

"Hello," she answered cautiously.

"Karen, this is your mother. I had a distant cousin in Oklahoma. She died and left me her farm and orchard. I'm going out there," Hannah said.

Karen was shocked and didn't speak for several seconds. "You had a cousin in Oklahoma? You never mentioned that."

"Doesn't matter now. I'm going. Just wanted you to know we'll be leaving this afternoon," Hannah said.

Karen picked up the pen. "What's your flight number?"

"Kim and I are driving."

"You are *what*?"

"Kim is going to rent us a car, and we're driving across country because I want to. Don't be trying to talk me out of it, because my mind is made up and a dozen angels dancing on a barbed-wire fence couldn't change it."

Karen held the phone out from her and stared at it. Her mother had never made a joke in her life. Was she beginning to suffer the first stages of Alzheimer's? Karen had heard that their personalities did a hundred-and-eighty-degree turnaround when that happened.

"How long are you staying?" she asked cautiously.

"Probably all summer. Maybe forever," Hannah said.

"Sounds like a harebrained idea to me. I'll come over and we'll talk about it."

"I don't care what kind of idea you think it is. I'm going and I'm not going to be in a hurry to come back. A corporation called me a few months ago with an offer to buy my hotel, and I might sell it to them at the end of the summer. I'll be living in Norma's house, which is now mine. It's a comfortable three-bedroom with indoor plumbing and air-conditioning these days. Are you going with us?" Hannah asked.

"Absolutely not," Karen exclaimed.

Oklahoma! What would she do?

"Then, I'll call Sue to tell her we're going. We'll be leaving as soon as the rental place can deliver a car if you change your mind. Kim can use her cell phone a couple of times a day to let you know we haven't been abducted by aliens or met up with hitchhiking serial killers."

Karen stared at the phone as if it were something foreign in her hand. Surely her mother hadn't just mentioned aliens and killers in the same breath. The pacing started again. Her mother was suffering dementia and Kim wasn't old enough to recognize the signs. She was needed, but mercy! Oklahoma! That wasn't anything but dirt and sky and lots of cows and Indian casinos. She couldn't go, could she?

The argument began as she continued to pace back and forth.

She was in the middle of a nasty divorce and she couldn't go out on an impromptu trip with no planning except to throw a few things in a suitcase and go.

On the other hand, the winery could very well run itself. There was a competent manager, and Daniel still kept his fingers in the production. The distance away from the whole sordid divorce affair would do her good. She wouldn't have to face the girls at the country club and the pity in their faces as they told her that she was better off without Daniel.

She reached for the phone and pushed the speed dial for her best friend, Peg. It rang six times before Peg answered breathlessly.

"Hello, Karen. Please don't tell me you're canceling our lunch date. I've already reserved a table for two at the club," Peg said.

"I won't be able to keep that lunch date, so you'd better cancel the reservation. I'm leaving in the next hour or so with my mother on a summer trip," she said.

"Where? You've got to be kidding me. Oh, no! Did you find out? Who told you?" Peg asked.

"Find out what? I opened my day planner and saw where we had a lunch date. What was it that you are afraid I'll find out?"

"Nothing. Nothing at all," Peg stammered.

The lightbulb in her head clicked like a blast of sun in the middle of a moonless night.

"You slept with Daniel, didn't you?" Karen asked coldly.

"Who told you?"

"You just did. Good-bye, Peg."

The phone rang again while she still held it in her hands.

"Hello." She expected to hear Peg's lame excuse on the other end.

Daniel talked fast and furious, his voice cold and full of anger. "You can't do this. I can't work with you. Tiffany won't stand for us sharing the vineyard and winery. She's young, Karen. Don't you remember what it was like to be young and in love?"

If he'd been standing in front of her she would have choked him with her bare hands until he turned blue, but she didn't have that choice. "Seems like I do remember something about that, but then it all went down the toilet pretty quick. Tiffany can live with it. There's only one of me for her to be jealous about. My list is longer. Deal with it or sell me your half."

"I hope you are miserable," Daniel smarted off.

"Why should the future be any different?"

The phone went dead in her hands.

That settled it! She opened her closet doors, took out a suitcase, and flipped through row after row of business suits. What did a woman take to a farm in Oklahoma? Finally, she phoned her mother.

"Don't leave without me. I'm trying to figure out what to pack," she said.

"One or two decent outfits for church on Sunday. It's a small rural church, so they aren't real fussy, and they wouldn't know Prada from Dillard's. The rest should be casual. Jeans. Shorts. T-shirts. I'm glad you're going with us," Hannah said.

"Thanks," Karen mumbled.

She tossed things haphazardly into the suitcase, filled another case with her toiletries from the bathroom, and dressed in jeans, a T-shirt, and sandals. When the cab arrived she was waiting on the front porch. She wasn't staying all summer. Two weeks, maximum. No way could she live any longer with what she'd put in one suitcase.

Sue DeHaven poured a cup of coffee and picked up the newspaper. It was the first day of summer, and she dreaded it. The second year since her husband, Jeff, had been killed in a tragic car accident when a drunk driver ran a red light. She'd rather be living with a rigid daily teaching schedule than facing three months of nothing.

The phone rang, and she reached for the cordless on the kitchen bar.

"Hello," she said, not even looking at the Caller ID window.

Daniel started off breathless, and when he took time to catch his breath, his words were so cold they would have frozen the hinges off the gate into Hades. "You have got to talk sense to your mother, Sue. She won't sell me her half of the vineyard and winery. I've offered a generous price and even given her the house. All I took out were my personal belongings. She could retire easily on what I'm willing to pay for her part of the business. After all, she is fifty-nine, and she could go see the world."

Sue giggled. "You gave her the house. That's a laugh, Daddy. It was her grandfather's home, not yours. How can you give her something that's always been hers? Maybe she doesn't want to see the world."

"Come on, Sue. She's not been so easy to live with and you know it," Daniel pleaded.

Sue ran her fingers through her light-brown hair that had been cut in one of those ragged styles that looked like she'd done it herself with pinking shears. "But she never cheated on you."

His voice changed into his sweet-talking one. The cajoling tone he used when he wanted something, like her vow not to tell her mother about the woman.

"Have a heart. Talk to her. She doesn't need the business and I do. She's being unreasonable."

"Sorry, Dad. Can't help you. The business is all that's kept her sane. She's been reasonable for forty years. Kept thinking you'd straighten up your wandering ways. You'd best keep Tiffany away from her. She might change the girl's mind about marrying you if she tells her about all your affairs."

"You're just like her. There's not a bit of my blood in you. Sometimes I wonder if you are even my child," he said viciously.

"You're just angry because for once Mother isn't looking the other way and you don't get your way. Work with her or sell out to her. Tiffany can live with it. And we could always do a DNA test if you want proof about my paternity."

"You won't talk to her?" Daniel asked.

"Sure, I'll talk to her. I'll tell her to do what she wants. When's the wedding? Are Kim and I invited?"

"I'll let you know," he said coldly.

"Good-bye, Dad." She gently laid the receiver down.

She sipped lukewarm coffee and scanned the *Daily Athenaeum*. The Federal Aviation Administration recently approved a $3.75 million grant for the Morgantown Municipal Airport. The grant would be used to conduct an airport master plan study, improve runway safety, and install apron lighting. It all had to do with wildlife protection, but it would be a good thing for her family. When Hannah or her mother, Karen, decided to fly, they caught a hop from the Municipal to DC. When her father Daniel flew, he had his own little plane. Had her father thought about a prenuptial agreement with Tiffany? If not, she might own his airplane as well as his part of the winery when she got tired of a man who was older than her father.

The phone rang again, and she turned the page to the next section as she picked it up—again, without looking at Caller ID. "Hello."

"Good morning, Sue. Karen, Kim, and I are driving to Oklahoma. You want to go with us?" Hannah asked.

Sue sat down with a plop and looked at the phone. It was her Nanna's sweet southern voice, but she couldn't have heard her right. "Why are you driving to Oklahoma?"

"Because my distant cousin Norma died and left me her farm, and I want to go. We're leaving at noon if you want to go too. Kim is leasing a van so we can keep it as long as we like," Hannah said as matter-of-factly as if she'd just told Sue what was on the hotel menu for the night.

"You had a cousin? You never told us you had relatives!"

"Never had the need to tell you about Norma. Now I have the need to go and the need to tell you about her. Let me know if you want to go. We plan to be gone all summer, but we could be back by the time school starts," Hannah said.

"Of course, I'm going if y'all are. I'll bring my van. Don't rent one. Nanna, are you sure you're up to a trip that far?"

"I'm not a hundred. Kim and I'll be waiting in the lobby. It'll take us four days to get there. I'm the one with the map and I'll be telling whoever's driving when to start in the mornings and stop at night. Don't pack anything fancy, because you are going to be working in dirt every day. Call your mother. Her staff can take care of your house while you are gone."

"Yes, ma'am," Sue almost saluted in the air.

"Don't be late," Hannah said.

"I wouldn't dream of it." Sue hung up and hit the speed dial button for her mother's phone.

"Has Nanna lost her mind?" she asked when she heard her mother answer.

"Seems that way, doesn't it? I'm in the hotel lobby. Just arrived. Left my one suitcase beside the front desk. If she's dropped off the mental deep end, I'll go back home. If not, I guess I'm going to Oklahoma. God only knows I need to get away from Morgantown for a while. You going?"

"I said we could take my van. Are we all crazy, Mother?"

"Could be. I left all my high-heeled shoes in the closet and brought sandals and a pair of athletic shoes. I'm in the elevator now, going up, fixing to get out."

"Karen Tarleton in Oklahoma with no Italian shoes? This is the craziest thing I've ever heard."

"Hey, one pair of sandals is Italian. The ones I brought to wear to church. Has she ever mentioned a cousin or this town called Emet to you?" Karen asked.

"Does it have a shopping mall?" Sue asked.

"Look it up on the net. I'll wait just a minute while you do." Karen leaned against the wall beside the elevator.

"Mother, it has a population of just over one hundred people. I don't think there's a shopping mall."

"Hope we don't have to drive far to a grocery store," Karen said.

"And you are actually going to this place for the whole summer?"

"Right now I'd visit Hades to get away from Daniel and his baby bride and all this fanfare around the divorce for a couple of weeks. Oklahoma can't be that hot or that bad."

"I'll be there with my suitcase and the van in an hour, then. I can't believe I'm actually doing this."

"Me either. I'm about to ring Nanna's doorbell. See you soon."

Sue sat in the chair another five minutes trying to figure out if she'd just dreamed the whole morning. Maybe she wasn't even awake. She pinched her arm and it hurt like the dickens, so she was alive and awake. She headed down the hallway to her bedroom, pulled a suitcase out of her closet, and packed according to what Hannah had said, except for a small black velvet case with pockets where she stored the few pieces of vintage jewelry she had collected.

Hannah opened her closet doors and flipped hangers to the left. She chose two linen dresses with matching short-sleeved jackets for church. Two pair of slacks and shirts to match for traveling. Underwear, makeup, toiletries. Anything else she needed she'd buy or do without. Besides, what she had would last until the end of summer, and the clock ticking loudly inside her clogged veins kept shouting that her time was running out.

The girls would insist that she have that surgery that the doctor talked about if they knew, but she'd made up her mind against it. She'd be eighty this summer and that was enough mileage out of one body. She had few friends left and most of them were in nursing homes; some didn't know her from Betty Boop when she visited. Hannah wasn't going to end up like that.

Norma had written a year ago that Emet was nothing more than an agricultural area these days. They'd even lost their post office and now got their mail from a rural route delivery out of Milburn. But she'd never forget Emet in the forties. She'd never forget that summer, or Norma. They'd formed a friendship in one week that had endured wars, births, deaths, disappointments, and joys. Norma had been one of her secrets, and now she was going back to face her demons, and sometime during the summer she fully well planned on telling her girls the whole story of what happened that summer during the war.

She had just snapped the suitcase when she heard the doorbell. She threw open the door to find Kim standing there for the second time.

"Your grandmother and mother are going with us. We don't need to rent a car. Sue is bringing hers and will drive for us."

"Nanna, are you still sure about this? I'll call the car rental and cancel the van, but I want to be sure before I pack," Kim said.

Hannah nodded seriously. "More than I've been about anything in my life. I've been on the phone with Roger, and he'll run things here at the hotel. I won't even be missed."

"Oklahoma, here we come. I can't believe we're all going together."

"Go pack." Hannah turned Kim around and pushed her toward the elevator.

Hannah was on her way back to the living room when the doorbell rang again. That would definitely be Karen. If Hannah had ever done anything right in her life, having the perfect daughter was the highlight of it all. Karen had married well, uniting her family with Daniel Tarleton's. He'd been brought up in the wine business just like Karen. Together they'd reorganized the Brewer Winery and taken it to new heights after Raymond Cosby died. Their wine was beyond criticism. Too bad Daniel wasn't. Who'd have thought when he was courting Karen that he'd turn out to be such a sorry rat? The faultless child Hannah and Jesse produced had been doomed to a terrible marriage. Hannah considered it the price for her own sins.

She opened the door to find Karen putting away her cell phone. Karen looked up with the pretty Brewer eyes. Jesse had marked his daughter, granddaughter, and great-granddaughter with his crystal-clear blue eyes. They all had different shades of hair, graduating from Karen's dark brown to Sue's light brown to Kim's almost blonde, but the blue eyes were the same.

Karen crossed the room and sat on the soft velvet sofa. "Sue wants to know if you've lost your mind."

"We'll see by the end of the summer. What else have the lot of you to do anyway? You can stay home and wallow around in the pity pool at the club. You can keep company with all those women who are commiserating with you one minute and snickering behind your back the next. Sue can stay home and putter around in her flower beds until she dies of boredom. Kim can help at the hotel like she's done every summer since she was big enough to walk or go run the computers for me in Oklahoma. Doesn't sound like any of you are giving up a lot to go with me."

"Well, I'm not looking forward to days and days in a van riding to Oklahoma. Let's at least have a change of heart and fly, Mother."

"It's got air-conditioning and bucket seats. Lots of legroom. You'll live. You might have Prada withdrawal, but we'll be your support team," Hannah teased. "Who knows, we may never come back and we'll need Sue's van to get us all around out there. Norma had a pickup truck. You want to ride in the back of the truck with no air-conditioning the whole time we are there and let that hot Oklahoma wind tangle up your hair? Not me! I'm riding up front in a van where it's cool, and so is Kim."

"You have definitely lost your mind. You don't make jokes." Karen eyed her gray-haired mother from across the room.

"If I did lose my mind, maybe I'll find it when I get where I'm going," Hannah said.

CHAPTER THREE

Hannah turned around in her seat and watched the hotel become smaller and smaller. When the last tree obliterated the sight of the tallest balcony, she looked ahead at the road. At least she wasn't crying like she did the first time she left Morgantown.

Mother and I boarded the train at noon that day. It was cool for June and we'd had a lot of rain, just like this year. I cried as I watched the familiar sights fade away and the future loom ahead like a fog. Mother sat stoically on the sofa in the private car and read a book as if we were going on a vacation. She could have refused to take me to Oklahoma, but Father's word was law.

Karen reached behind her and grabbed a pillow. She fluffed it up and stuck it against the window. Four days was a lot of hours, and she fully well planned to sleep most of them. She shut her eyes but she didn't sleep. What in the devil was she doing? She wasn't impulsive. She didn't wake up one morning and say, "I'm going to Oklahoma for three months to a hot, dusty farm." She was so methodical that Daniel had often said he could set his clock to the second by her schedule. She kept a calendar and an appointment book. Everything except her disastrous marriage was set in stone. She was a clone of her grandfather, Raymond Cosby, who bottled his first wine from the Brewer Winery before she was born.

Daniel Tarleton has no right to that label. It was mine from the time I could walk behind Grandfather in the vineyards. It's mine as much as the house is.

Karen replayed the story of her marriage with her eyes shut.

The courtship had been truly awesome. Daniel was smooth, kind, romantic, and everything a girl could want. It lasted six months and then he proposed. Even that was out of a storybook. Down on one knee in the grape arbor, ring in hand, telling her how much he loved her.

Ten months later Susanna Kay was born. She was supposed to be Daniel Franklin Tarleton IV, not a six-pound bald girl with a pug nose, but he had loved her. She had to give him credit for loving his daughter even if his love for his wife had waned by the time the baby was born.

For sixteen years, Karen threw her heart and soul into making a life for Sue. Then she threw up her hands and left Sue at home that summer when she went to Italy. When she returned, she found a quiet, subdued sixteen-year-old child in the place of the feisty, headstrong teenager she'd left behind. The new kid studied hard, went to college on scholarships, and refused to take a dime of Brewer money from her parents.

Sue dated Jeff DeHaven, a good kid from a lower-middle-class family, all through her senior year of high school and eloped with him just before they started college. They were both eighteen, so Karen couldn't do a thing about it.

Kim was born a year later. Karen offered to hire a nanny, but Sue refused. She and Jeff alternated their schedules so one of them would keep her while the other attended classes, and they both worked at minimum-paying jobs to support their young family.

Karen finally drifted off to sleep, only to dream of that summer when she went to Italy: the happiest three weeks of her life.

Hannah hummed some kind of unrecognizable song. Karen snored, more like a purr than a real honest-to-God snore. Kim read a thick romance novel. Sue kept her eyes on the road. Hannah had said they'd travel south to Huntington, on the other end of West Virginia, where they'd stop for the night at whatever hotel was close to the highway. From there she wanted to take a two-lane highway through most of Kentucky and Missouri. For reasons only she knew, she wanted to be able to see the railroad tracks as much as possible.

It was the first time Sue could ever remember the four of them being in a car together going anywhere. There were a few times when they vacationed together. Times when she'd swallowed her enormous pride and let her mother and grand-mother pay for trips to New York, once to France and a couple to resort areas like Cancun or the Bahamas. But to get in a van and go? Never.

She glanced over at her daughter, Kim. She and Jeff had wanted a house full of children. But after Kim, there were no more. They had planned to see a specialist, but then the years went by and they never did.

Sue focused on the road, but it didn't keep her mind from straying back in time.

It must be the fact that Nanna kept a secret from us that has me thinking about the past. Everything changed that summer when Mother went to Italy. Up until then I heard Mother and Daddy fighting, mostly about his flirting. And then he brought that woman home while she was gone and everything fell apart after that. It was as if she was blind, because she never fought with him about it again and it got worse and worse. Of course, that was the summer that Corky died. I should have told Mother about Corky, but what could she have done or said? It was done and over and my fault. I still think of him when I smell English Leather shaving lotion or see a cocky young man strutting down the school hallway.

What had dredged up those old memories? The heavy silence in the minivan? How on earth were the four of them going to survive a whole summer together if they couldn't find anything to discuss the first two hours of the trip?

Kim remembered to turn a page every so often so the other three would think she was really reading. Looking back, they'd never talked much. Not about anything other than business, school, and such. No one had ever said, "Hey, remember back when…" and told a long story. She was glad her great-grandmother had dropped the bombshell on them about going away for the whole summer. Anywhere was fine with her as long as she couldn't possibly bump into Marshall when she was at the mall or the country club. Strange how they'd both belonged to the same circles and yet had never met until a few months ago.

She knew exactly what night she'd gotten pregnant. It was the only night she'd been married, so she figured up the due date and found out she'd be having a baby at the end of February. It was strange to think about the fifth generation having a birthday party in the middle of the winter. All four of the Brewer women had summer birthdays.

Good Lord, tomorrow is Nanna's birthday. Neither of them can call the florist and have a dozen roses delivered to the van as we drive down the highway. What on earth will we do? I'll have to remind them when we stop tonight so we can plan something. I bet Grandma didn't even bring a bottle of vintage wine in her suitcase. Oh, well, we'll have to hit a liquor store for champagne at the least, or a good restaurant. And this one should be a special birthday since she'll be eighty. I'll wait until after that to tell them I'm pregnant. Shock like that would be a lousy birthday present.

She chanced a look over her shoulder at Hannah, who was watching the lovely mountainous scenery go by at nearly seventy miles an hour. Her silver hair was cut close to her neckline, feathered back over her ears, and styled with light bangs about halfway to her dark eyebrows. Hannah Brewer always said she'd never have gray eyebrows; they made a woman look older than her years. She could have walked out of an advertisement in the AARP magazine in her pale blue slacks, matching cotton sweater, and white sandals.

Karen slept until just before noon and awoke more relaxed than she'd been in years. "Want me to drive a spell?"

"I'm still good," Sue said. "You getting tired, Nanna?"

"No, but I'm hungry. There's a sign for a Burger King. Take the next exit and we'll have burgers and fries," she said.

"What?" Karen sputtered.

"They probably have some kind of salad, darlin' daughter. If not, order a hamburger, take the meat off, put it on my burger, and eat the lettuce and tomatoes," Hannah said.

"I can't believe—" Karen started.

"Seems like I've heard that line so much already today that it is already old," Hannah said. "We are stopping for greasy burgers and fries. We can find a Walmart or a grocery store later and buy some antacids if we get heartburn."

"Yes, ma'am," Kim said loudly. "Burger King it is. Here we come."

And I hope today is not the day I decide to start that morning sickness stuff.

Sue, forever the peacekeeper, looked in the rearview mirror. "There's a Subway, Mother."

"Burgers and fries it is. Your nanna says so," Karen said.

"Don't sulk. I'll let you choose another day," Hannah said.

"I am not sulking," Karen declared.

Hannah giggled. "Yeah, you are, but I kind of like it. It beats that submissive woman who came home from Italy all those years ago. What ever happened there?"

"Like you said, that's a story for another day," Karen said.

Kim giggled nervously. "Sounds like when another day gets here we're going to have lots of stories."

They had a quick lunch and were back on the road in less than half an hour.

"Sometimes I can catch a glimpse of the railroad tracks running along beside us. We're going the right way," Hannah said.

"What's the railway got to do with the route?" Kim asked.

"I might tell you someday when I get where I'm going," Hannah said.

"Tell us a story now, Nanna, not another day," Kim begged. "Entertain us. I don't remember you ever talking about yourself when you were a little girl. Did Poppa Raymond ever talk about her, Grandmother?" Kim turned around in the seat to look at Karen.

"He just said she was a pretty little girl," Karen said.

Hannah jerked her head around to look at Karen. "My father said that?"

"One time not long before he died, I asked him to tell me a story about you. He said you were a pretty little girl with big blue eyes and pretty blonde hair. That's all I could get out of him."

Hannah smiled. "Hmmmph. How interesting."

"Why, Nanna? Didn't he ever tell you that?" Sue asked.

"No, don't remember that he did. I always had the feeling I was a big disappointment because I was a girl. He wanted a son so badly, and then Mother couldn't have any more children after me. I think he would have kept his interest in the railroad if I'd been a boy, but women didn't run such businesses back then, so he sold out and started the vineyard as a hobby. Then he bought the hotel. Worked out for the best, I suppose. He was kind enough to give Jesse and me the hotel when we married."

Sue patted Kim on the arm. "Your father loved you."

"And so did yours," Karen said.

"Maybe when I was a little girl. I don't think he loves me much today," Sue said.

"Oh?" Karen raised an eyebrow.

"We had an argument. He called me before we left. Wanted me to talk to you, and I told him he was wrong and you were right. I don't think he was too happy with me, because he said he doubted that I was even his child," Sue said.

"He's just angry because for the first time I'm not letting him have his way," Karen told her and then looked out the side window again.

Kim wondered if she carried a boy or a girl. At least she wouldn't have a husband to care which one was born next February.

Hannah gazed out the window again.

Yes, he gave us the hotel, but it was in Jesse's name, not mine. It was Jesse's payment for marrying me, for taking on the responsibility. It didn't become my hotel until Jesse died. So he thought I was a pretty little girl? At least there's that.

They reached Huntington at four thirty. Sue was surprised to see that they'd driven 212 miles. "Well, I guess this is the first night's stop. Where's the best hotel in town? Shall we stop and ask, or do you know, Nanna?"

"Super 8 is right there. It'll do," Hannah said cheerfully.

"Super 8?" Karen was aghast. "You *have* lost your mind. There must at least be a Ramada or a Holiday Inn? Maybe a nice bed and breakfast?"

"Super 8." Hannah handed her credit card over Sue's shoulder. "You go inside and get us two rooms—with an adjoining door would be nice, but if they haven't got that, then at least on the same floor."

Karen raised her perfectly arched dark eyebrows another inch. "Two rooms?"

"Yes, two rooms. We'll draw straws or arm wrestle for who shares. Sue, tell them we want two beds in each room. At least you get your own bed, Karen, now stop whining."

"I'm not whining. I just can't believe you are staying in a Super 8. Are we eating at McDonald's tonight?"

Hannah laughed out loud. "No, we're ordering pizza brought to the room. You can choose whatever kind you want. I'm having a supreme with extra bell peppers," Hannah said.

Karen rolled her eyes. "The answer is yes, Sue. She has definitely lost her mind. Why, Mother?"

"Because I'm calling the shots and I want more junk food," Hannah told them. "Tomorrow before we leave town, we're finding a Walmart. I'm buying some overalls and a couple of T-shirts."

"Are you joking?" Sue unfastened the seat belt.

Hannah shook her head seriously. "You better all buy either jeans or overalls and cheap T-shirts too. It's dusty and dirty in a vegetable garden. And there are no housekeepers at Norma's house either. We'll be taking care of the house, the garden, the canning, making pickles and jelly, and selling all that plus the produce in the fruit stand. Plus there's the irrigation and picking vegetables every morning and cleaning them and putting them in baskets to sell and all the other work. We'll go to bed tired and get up tired most of the summer. Oh, and there are two old donkeys and a couple of feeder calves in the back lot."

"How do you know about orchards and gardens? And what are feeder calves?" Kim asked.

"Feeder calves are two young calves that she buys from Luke every year to raise up for butchering. Norma says the donkeys stay with them because they keep the coyotes from attacking her winter pot roasts, but the real reason is that they have been on the farm for a long time and she's attached to those ugly creatures. The rest is a long story. One to be told after a hard day's work, with a glass of lemonade in one hand and a fat bologna sandwich in the other. A sandwich with mayonnaise, lettuce, and ripe tomatoes right from the garden."

"And why are we doing this?" Karen asked.

"Because I want to," Hannah said. "Here comes Sue. Guess she had some luck, because she's carrying those silly credit-card door-openers. I fought Jesse on that. He wanted to install that kind of thing, but not me. I still think folks like a real key."

"It gets expensive rekeying the locks when they take the keys or lose them," Karen said.

"Brewer Hotel has never worked in the red yet. There's enough money in the bank account to keep all four of us until the day the preacher talks us into heaven. I hope he's very convincing," Hannah said.

Karen sighed. Hannah was making jokes and talking about buying overalls and insisting they all stay in a middle-class hotel when God only knew they could afford the best of the best. Not to mention the humor. Maybe she had a brain tumor in addition to early-stage dementia.

Sue started up the van and pulled out from under the front awning to a parking space. "It's early, so they had two rooms on the ground floor with a connecting door. Why did you want that, Nanna? We are to go through the front doors, and the rooms are right around the corner to the left. There's doughnuts and coffee in the morning if we are interested."

"I wanted it so we could leave the doors open and visit. Forget the continental breakfast. We'll have breakfast at McDonald's. Bacon, cheese, and egg biscuits with hash browns. My little fat cells are already happy just thinking about it," Hannah said.

Karen groaned. "I won't be able to fasten my slacks in a week's time."

"It won't matter. Overalls have a nice big comfortable waist," Hannah said.

Kim grabbed her suitcase from the back and popped the handle up to roll it inside. "Then overalls it is. How hot is it in Oklahoma at this time of year? Isn't it where they put all the Indians way back when? Reckon we'll see any of them?"

Maybe she could hide the thickening waist awhile if she wore overalls and T-shirts. She was about six weeks: it would be a couple of months before she could expect even the slightest bulge, and overalls might buy her some time.

"It's hotter than Lucifer's tail feathers this time of year," Hannah told her. "If it drops below a hundred degrees the old-timers call it a cold snap. I don't know about Indians other than Luke O'Neal, the rancher who lives south of Norma, has a little bit in him. She says you'd never know it to look at him though. His momma had long dark hair and brown eyes. She died in a car crash when he was about two, and his dad was in the military, so his grandparents raised him. His dad was killed in some mission in a third-world country when Luke was ten or eleven. Anyway, he doesn't look a bit Indian. He looks like his Irish dad and has fair skin, blue eyes, and blond hair. Norma hires a couple of high school kids to help her gather vegetables in the spring and fruit in the summer, but we are going to run the place without any extra help."

It was more words than they'd ever heard out of Hannah at one time.

"How do you know all this?" Sue helped Hannah with her suitcase.

"Norma and I kept in touch through the years," Hannah said.

When they were inside their rooms, Hannah crawled up into the middle of the bed inside their room and crossed her legs Indian-style. "See, all hotel rooms look basically the same. A bed, nightstand, lamps, table, television set, and a chair or two."

"Except that there are satin sheets on the beds at the Brewer, mints on the pillows, fresh flowers on the tables, a gorgeous view of the West Virginia mountains, and a restaurant with a hot breakfast instead of doughnuts and coffee," Karen reminded her mother.

"Ten-dollar breakfast, two-dollar flowers, and a fifty-cent mint at three times the cost. You're buying style at the Brewer. We're buying a place to sleep and visit right here. Tomorrow night I may choose one of those old 1950s-style hotels. The kind that are long and low and face a concrete courtyard with weeds in the center flower bed where a fountain used to be."

"Whew, Nanna, whatever bug crawled up your hind end has sure enough got us all worried about you." Kim laughed.

Hannah laughed with her.

It's me. The real me. The one who went this route more than sixty years ago. I left that girl in Oklahoma and I'm going back to get her. You ain't seen nothing yet, honey. Just wait and keep your eyes open.

Hannah handed the brochure from the nightstand to her daughter. "Karen, you order the pizza. I want a small supreme with double bell peppers, and ask them to send a couple of those big bottles of Coke. Not diet. The real thing. You other two better be thinking about what you want. It's been a long time since my hamburger at lunch, and I'm starving. Oh, order up a big order of those cheese bread sticks too, in case we get hungry later tonight. Kim, you take that trash can right there and find the ice machine. Fill it up."

"Trash can?" Kim cocked her head to one side.

"Honey, it's got a plastic liner in it. Made out of the same stuff as the liner in that silly little two-cup bucket. By the way, I vote that Karen sleeps in here with me and you other two can share the room through there," Hannah told her.

"Whatever you say, Mother. This is your trip, although I'm beginning to believe it's a trip in more ways than one," Karen said.

Hannah's green eyes twinkled. "Oh, as in when the young people smoke that grass stuff and trip out? Well, we're not doing illegal stuff in here. Lord, can't you just see the newspaper at home if we got caught tripping in this hotel? Headlines would read, 'Brewer women trade wine for joints.' Now that would cause a stir in polite circles, wouldn't it? I bet it would even get Daniel and Twinkle Toes thrown out of the country club."

"Where is my mother? What have you done with her? Did the aliens steal her and put you in her body?" Karen laughed. "And it's Tiffany, not Twinkle Toes."

"Tomato. Tomahto. Bimbo or Bim…bo! All the same," Hannah said.

"Sue, darlin', *your* grandmother has shown the first signs of a sense of humor in her whole life. Come quickly and don't miss the miracle," Karen yelled through the door.

Sue's giggles answered her.

Hannah picked up the pizza brochure and threw it at Karen. "I get worse when I'm hungry. Pizza in thirty minutes or I begin to froth at the mouth and throw myself on the floor."

Karen dialed the number and put in an order for four small pizzas: one cheese for her and one sausage for Sue, one supreme for Hannah, one black olive for Kim. It was the first time she knew that Kim liked black olives. Daniel liked them, but she'd always thought they looked like eyeballs from strange alien creatures. Maybe that's what was wrong with Hannah. She'd eaten a whole bottle of black olives this morning before breakfast and they'd affected her ability to think clearly.

They sat on the two beds and ate pizza with their fingers, drank Coke from plastic cups they'd dug out of sealed wrappers in the bathrooms, wiped their hands on paper napkins, and watched reruns from the second season of *Law and Order*.

"Look at those smart women. I could have been a cop or a lawyer," Hannah tossed her pizza box at the trash can and missed.

Kim licked the last of the cheese from her fingertips. "Why weren't you? You were certainly smart enough to run a hotel back when all the books were kept by hand. I bet you would have been a good lawyer."

Hannah smiled. "Women could keep books for their husbands. They could even be lawyers back in the forties, but not like those women," Hannah said during the five-minute commercial break. "There were socially accepted things and then there were those that weren't. I could keep books and oversee the cleaning staff. My ideas, like putting flowers in the rooms, or little things to make it a classy joint, weren't tossed out with the breakfast scraps, but…"

How much did she say right then? It wasn't time yet to spring the whole story on them. They'd had only one day to see the girl she'd taken to Oklahoma and left there more than sixty years before.

"But what, Nanna?" Sue asked.

"There are no *ifs* or *buts* when you are almost eighty, darlin'," Hannah told her. "There are only *and*s, and I'm not ready to tell y'all the *and* part of my life. Here's the show again. They'll nail that son of a gun before it's over, and I don't mean the one on the stand. He's innocent as a newborn lamb."

Karen shook her head.

Sue's eyes widened. Did Hannah have a brain tumor?

Kim was skating on totally unfamiliar territory. Pregnant. Terrified. And now all this change with her family, who'd been rock solid in their stuffiness her whole life.

"Then who do you think the culprit is?" Sue asked.

"Oh, it's the doorman to the hotel," Hannah said. "He's the one who'd have access to the apartment, and he's got a shifty look in his eyes. I know that kind of man. I've fired dozens of them."

"Oh, Nanna, you never fired anyone." Kim laughed.

"Not in person. Jesse did it when he was alive, and when he died I hired a manager who did it for me. But never think that I don't know a worthless culprit when I see one. Does that sound better than horse crap, Karen? I know I've offended your delicate nature all too much today."

Karen bowed up. "I'm not delicate."

"Well, halle-dang-lujah," Hannah singsonged. "I'd begun to think Daniel and his thumb-sucking baby doll could talk you out of anything. I didn't think you'd show up to go today.

I'm glad to see you're not delicate. I hope we can toughen you up even more this summer."

"I'm as tough as the rest of you. Just because Grandpa left me the big house and gave the winery to me and Daniel doesn't mean I've wallowed in the lap of luxury. I've worked as hard as anyone here. Sue lived in that house until she graduated, so she had eighteen years of being spoiled too," Karen argued.

"Yes, but she refused it after a while. We'll see if there's a tough woman under all that Prada and beauty parlor help," Hannah said.

"What about you, Mother?" Karen protested. "*You* live in the lap of luxury. A three-bedroom penthouse. Anything you want carried to you at any time of the night or day."

Hannah looked away from the television and then back at it. "It's time we all got to know each other a lot better. Look, I told you that sorry sucker was the culprit. Now we'll see if they've got enough evidence to hang him."

Later that night Karen stretched out in a queen-sized bed with cotton sheets. She couldn't remember the last time she'd slept in anything but a California king with satin sheets.

Her mother slept soundly, if it could be judged by the soft snoring. What other secrets were hidden in her Hannah's past? Evidently, she'd been to Oklahoma at some time, but it had never been mentioned.

Hannah awoke before dawn. It took several minutes for her to get her bearings and realize why her bedroom had changed. Tears ran down her cheeks as she thought about Norma. She'd miss her so much. For more than sixty years they'd carried on a friendship through letters and phone calls, and now there would be no more of her colorful anecdotes about her neighbor, John, or that handsome young man, Luke, who lived on the other side of her farm. No more tales of the blistering-hot summers and the fear that the crop would be a disaster.

And—there was that word again—there'd be no one for Hannah to write to when she was sad or joyful. No outlet for her own emotions. She mourned the girl she'd lived with that one week, the one whose friendship she'd cherished for more than half a century.

Today they'd cremate Norma, and on her birthday in August, Hannah was scattering Norma's ashes over the fields.

She felt a peace that superseded all the tears. Hannah was going home to finish her life. She wiped away the tears and remembered that today she was eighty years old and she was about to let the hidden secrets in the past out of the closet. Her perfect daughter, granddaughter, and great-granddaughter might as well know. Then when the angels came calling for her soul, she could tell them that she had nothing to hide and go sliding right up to the gates of heaven with a big smile on her face.

With the back of her veined hand, she wiped away the tears, then she got up and, for the first time in decades, made her own coffee in the little maker beside the sink. The aroma of it brewing filled the room and smelled absolutely wonderful.

CHAPTER FOUR

Luke crawled up in his tractor and shut the door. Those horrible women would arrive later today. He could hardly bear the idea of them living in Norma's house and owning her things, feeding Buster and Sparky, and running the fruit stand. That fruit stand had been a landmark as much as the Chickasaw White House in Emet. It took a special breed to run a fruit stand, day in and day out. Those highfalutin women wouldn't be able to stand the heat. He didn't care how much faith Norma put in them.

She'd talked about them constantly, but if there was such a strong bond, why in the devil had he never met any of them? He'd lived right next door to her his whole life. He was born in the house he lived in now. He had walked the fence line on the 320 acres he owned since his great-grandpa died a year ago so many times that he couldn't count them. One of his fondest memories was sneaking through the fence and riding the donkeys like horses when he was a young boy. Norma didn't care if he was an Indian or a cowboy and the donkeys didn't ask if he was Superman on horseback or Batman. All those wonderful memories, and these women on their way to claim her farm had never come to see her.

Did they think they were too good for the likes of Norma, with her truck, farm, and fruit stand? Anybody that was too good for her wasn't good enough for him. He dreaded having to deal with them, but he'd promised her that he'd be helpful if she went before he did.

He smiled at that, but that's the way she always said it: "if I go first" he was to do this or that. Statistics said that she'd go first. But Norma never believed statistics. She said the good Lord had things under control and He'd take care of it all when the time was right. It was like she knew something Luke didn't. Well, by golly, one thing he did know, he wasn't going to like those hoity-toity women.

He got into his truck and headed for the feed store in Durant for a load of chicken feed. When he got back, maybe the women would have already turned tail in their high-heeled shoes and fancy power suits and lit a shuck back to West Virginia. A man could surely hope, couldn't he?

"History is dead wrong," Sue exclaimed as she drove through a tiny town called Tishomingo, Oklahoma, and headed east. "The world is not round. It is flat, and we just drove off the edge."

Hannah smiled and nodded.

"Where are you taking me, Mother? I can't live here. I feel like I'm on the top of a mountain about to fall off the side any minute. There's nothing but dirt and sky." Hannah remembered saying those words, but the landscape wasn't totally flat. It wasn't the beautiful West Virginia mountains, but it did have rolling hills. Sue and Kim would adapt. Karen would

either wilt like yesterday's hibiscus or bloom all summer like a marigold.

"We're almost there, another eleven or twelve miles," she said after a minute of scary silence as the other three looked around them at the desolate surroundings: two red lights, a couple of clothing stores, a few convenience stores, a church, and one grocery store down the street from the funeral home. "Just to forewarn you, Tishomingo is a hub of activity compared to Emet. We'll reach Milburn next and then south to Emet, where there's not even a grocery store or a post office anymore."

Karen moaned.

Sue gasped.

Kim giggled. "Yes, but are you aware that Blake Shelton and Miranda Lambert live between Tishomingo and Milburn? I was watching a video of them last night on CMT and I couldn't believe they live in Oklahoma."

"Who's that?" Karen asked.

"Just the two hottest country music stars on the charts," Kim said.

"By whose standard?" Sue asked.

"Mine! I hope someday I happen to run into them in a grocery store, or in that bar." Kim pointed at a small beer joint on the north side of the road.

"You stay out of that place," Hannah said.

"Then work some magic and let Blake and Miranda go to the church where Norma went."

Hannah pointed to the left. "That's it right there."

"Nanna, that is so small," Sue said.

"Yes, but God don't have to have a cathedral to send his spirit to on Sunday. There's a sharp curve coming up. Slow down."

Three miles later they passed the city limits sign for Emet, Oklahoma, on one end of a tiny community and then passed it again on the other end.

"Is that it? Is this really a town?" Karen asked.

"That's it. Keep going straight, Sue. We'll turn left in a mile or so. The old oak tree was hit by lightning about thirty years ago. Norma said that there isn't even a twig left of it, but there is the fruit stand. Turn down that lane right there beside it. That'll be Norma's house. You can see it from here." Hannah was so excited that Sue looked in the rearview to see her face.

"*Deliverance* is reality," Karen said.

"I rented that movie a couple of years ago. Scared the bejesus out of me. Emet isn't like that at all," Hannah said.

"I can't get used to this new you," Sue said.

Kim looked over the back of the front seat at her grandmother. "I can't get used to those clothes."

Hannah wore a pair of stretch denim capris she'd bought at Walmart and a bright red T-shirt with a big yellow rose on the front. Her two-dollar flip-flops and baseball cap were the same shade as the bird. Silver hair, usually styled perfectly, had been washed and let go for four days and looked like it had been combed with an electric knife.

"I'm comfortable in my skin," Hannah declared. "And slow down. See the orchard south of the house? And the garden is out behind the house and the donkeys and calves in a pasture behind that and the barn is back there with them. Oh, my! It's exactly the way I remember it, other than a new house."

Karen sucked air. "No air-conditioning? Nanna, it'll be very hot in that fruit stand. Who's going to sit out there and sell stuff?"

"I will if none of you will, but I'm thinking that will be Kim's job."

Sue slowed down to a stop.

An old red pickup truck sat in the driveway. A riot of color overflowed the flower beds: yellow, red, pink, purple, blue. It looked as if God had thrown every color he could find into the yard.

"We are home!" Hannah said.

It was a long, one-story ranch-style house with a deep front porch surrounded with another spray of color. While they climbed out of the car and stretched their tired muscles, the sprinkler system popped up and began to shoot water.

"I wondered how they got things to grow in this miserable heat. This place is hotter'n Hades, Mother. I can smell smoking brimstone."

Sue grabbed suitcases from the back and sneezed. "Smell it. I can feel it. I could sunburn just walking from here to the house. Dirt. I hate dirt in my nose."

Hannah laughed. "Well, get used to it. You'll be snorting a lot of it. And just between me and thee, I don't think the Lord gives a flip about how bad you hate dirt in your nose. Aren't the flowers beautiful? Norma liked her flowers. Said she'd have them when she was living instead of when she was dead. The sprinkler system was my idea."

"Is there a key?" Sue asked.

"John left it under the doormat." Hannah stepped around the water spray, picked up the edge of a rough brown welcome mat, found the key, and opened the door.

An eerie feeling met them in the foyer of unfamiliar territory. On the left a half brick wall with wooden spindles at the top gave them a view of an enormous kitchen. Six chairs sat around an oak table with a shiny oak wagon wheel chandelier hanging above it. Beyond that a bar formed a big U-shaped kitchen. The whole area was papered in bright yellow roses, and lacy curtains hung in the windows over white miniblinds.

Hannah ignored the kitchen and marched straight ahead to the living area. The whole back wall was glass, floor to ceiling, looking out at a backyard full of flowers and pecan trees. A natural stone fireplace with a six-inch mantel took up most of the north end of the room. A dark green velvet sofa with deep cushions and matching chairs faced the cold fireplace. The other end of the room held a baby grand piano and a doorway into a hallway, where they located two closets, one bathroom, and three bedrooms.

Hannah turned quickly to find all three girls right behind her. She pointed to the first room on her left. "I'm sleeping in this one. It was Norma's room and I want to be among her things. Sue, put my suitcases and bags in here. Kim, you can have the one across the hall, right here. Sue and Karen can share the one with twin beds."

"Twin beds?" Karen whined.

"You'll be sixty years old this summer. If the worst thing you ever have to do between now and the day you have to sweep the golden streets of heaven is sleep in a twin bed for a few weeks, you'll be blessed, indeed," Hannah told her.

Hannah had known from the time she left Morgantown exactly what the sleeping arrangements would be. She'd take the room Norma had used because the letters were in the closet. Sue and Karen needed to get to know each other. Something happened when Karen went to Italy and that young boy was killed in a car accident. Whatever it was had changed the course of their lives, and they needed time together in a small space to get it sorted out.

"Oh, come on, it'll be fun. We can talk about them," Sue teased.

Karen opened her mouth to say something, but she suddenly realized she didn't know enough about her mother or granddaughter to talk about them.

"Hello," a masculine voice called from the living room, "you ladies here?"

Hannah yelled back. "That you, John?"

"Yes, ma'am. It's me."

Hannah extended her hand when they reached the living room. "I'm Hannah and I'm glad to meet you. Norma talked a lot about you."

John shook hands with her. "Thank you. She was a pistol, but I loved that old girl. And y'all four is about all she talked about, especially this last while."

John's smile seemed sincere, and Kim liked him on first impression. Karen saw a working man, not totally unlike any of the dozen or more gardeners in her employ. The old straw hat he laid on the coffee table reminded her of the one she wore when she went to the flower beds to work off an anger fit, most usually at Daniel.

Sue was glad she didn't have to speak. John stirred emotions she thought she'd burned back when she was sixteen. He reminded her of Corky. Medium height. Skin browned from spending too much time in the sun. Full mouth. Beautiful smile. Muscles bulging against the fabric of a faded red T-shirt.

John drew a wooden chair from beside the fireplace to the seating arrangement. "I've been in the fields all day. I'm too dirty to sit on Miss Norma's furniture."

Hannah nodded and pointed at the other women. "John, meet my family. This is my daughter, Karen. My granddaughter, Sue. And my great-granddaughter, Kim. We are going to stay for the summer."

"I'm glad. I have no idea what to do with that computer. I know there'll be bills due by the first of next month. I think she paid them just before she died." His Adam's apple bobbed twice before he spoke again.

"She spoke of you often, Miz Hannah, and left me the letter telling me what to do when she died. We just weren't expecting it to come right now."

"What happened?" Karen asked.

"Heart attack. The doctor said she was dead long before she hit the floor that morning. I found her, called the ambulance, and they came, but it was too late," John said hoarsely.

"Where is a hospital?" Karen asked.

"Durant. She had a regular doctor at the Milburn Family Clinic and a heart specialist down in Durant. The doctor said it wouldn't have mattered who I called. She'd been gone an hour or more when I found her. I was glad they told me she hadn't suffered," John said.

"Me too," Hannah said. "That's the second-best way to go. The only better way is to go to sleep and never wake up. Now what's going on here?"

John nodded seriously. "She'd made arrangements to be cremated, so that's taken care of. Her ashes are up there on the mantel. She said you'd know what to do." He pointed.

Kim shivered.

He went on, "She said you'd know when the time was right. The computer is in there." He pointed to a door beside the fireplace that none of them had noticed. "It's her office, and in the letter to me, she said to tell Kim what she needs is in the desk drawer in a little notebook."

Hannah reached across and patted him on the shoulder. "Thank you. Norma's last letter said the crop was looking good. Is that still so?"

"This year could well be her best in more than a decade. Norma was excited about it. Rain has been perfect. Not too much heat."

"What was that again about the heat?" Karen asked.

"Hasn't been a bad year, yet. Only had a couple of days it reached a hundred degrees. Mostly been staying in the nineties and we've had good rain. She's been irrigating three times a week, though."

"Have the lawyers been called?" Hannah asked.

"Don't need to be. Not really. Somehow she set it up so it would go directly to you. They'll be around in a day or two to explain it. Harper, Stillman, and Wesley out of Tishomingo. Tillman Harper was the only one she'd deal with. He's semi-retired and lives on a ranch between here and Milburn. I called him the day she died. He said to let him know when you arrived and he'd come over to explain the will sometime next week, but to just make yourselves at home. It's ironclad, but the gist is you inherited the whole place."

"Why'd she leave it to my mother?" Karen asked.

"Who knows why? She must have had her reasons, and, believe me, I'd trust her with my life, so I'd sure trust her judgment. She said you were the best friend she ever had. She said the letters are where they're supposed to be. She sure looked forward to your letters. They came right after the first of every month and sometimes even more often. She talked about Karen and Sue and Kim like they were her own kids.

Why didn't she ever go see you or why didn't y'all come out here?" John asked.

"It's a long story. A very long one for another day. We'll get unpacked and Kim can get to work on that computer," Hannah said.

"I'll be around after supper to check on things," John said. "The freezer is full. Almost a whole beef and two hogs. I figured you might be here today so I made sure there was fresh milk and eggs in the fridge. Cabinets are stocked. Oh, and the cellar…let me show you how to get to it."

He moved the heavy coffee table to one side without straining a single muscle, pulled back a rug, and lifted a door right in the middle of the floor. Steps led down into a cellar.

"It's a combination storm shelter, place to store the canning, wine cellar, and everything. She keeps…kept…you know what I mean—the potatoes, carrots, beets, and all, down there in bushel baskets."

Hannah peered down the black hole. "Do we need to harvest the garden in the morning?"

"Yes, ma'am. Beans are coming off faster than she could eat them or can them. There's two bushels in the kitchen waiting to get ready for the stand. You are going to keep it running, aren't you? Folks around here buy a lot from it," John said.

"Where's the light?" Hannah asked.

"First step. Reach over to your right. There's a switch. Got hurricane lamps full of oil in case the electricity goes out."

"And John, that fruit stand will be open every day except Sunday all summer long. Bring Luke around to meet us sometime. Norma talked a lot about him and you," Hannah said.

John nodded. "I'll be getting back home now. Call me if you need anything."

Hannah flipped the switch. "Come on, girls. This is an experience you don't want to miss."

They followed her down the steep stairs to the cool room below the house. An old plaid sofa flanked by beat-up end tables sat on one end. Across the entire northern wall were jars and jars of jellies, jams, and canned fruit. They were all labeled neatly, and boxes of new jars were shelved on the fourth wall.

"Look at all these jellies and jams. I want to try my hand at this," Karen said.

"I figured you'd want to use the grapes to make wine," Hannah said.

"No, I want to do something altogether different. Ever since you mentioned the fruit stand I've been thinking about my own label for fancy jam and jelly," she said.

Sue could scarcely believe her eyes. "It's a grocery store."

"Norma wasn't much on store-bought things. Milk, because after her father died, she swore she'd never milk another cow. Flour and sugar, that kind of thing. Mostly she raised what she ate," Hannah said. "I bet her recipes are around here somewhere."

Karen sat down on the threadbare sofa. "Mother, who is...was...this Norma, and why didn't you mention her?"

"Or John?" Sue asked.

"Or Luke?" Kim chimed in.

"Norma first," Karen said.

Hannah sat down beside Karen. "Her father was a third cousin to my father. That branch of the family left West Virginia back during the Civil War years and moved out here. I never knew they existed until that summer. Just before my seventeenth birthday. Actually, I spent that birthday right here on this spot. Norma had that place torn down about twenty years ago and built this one. Mother and I came out here on the train and then went home a week later. That house was bigger. Old rambling two-story, but it sat right here and Norma and I shared a bedroom upstairs."

"Why didn't you tell us about her?" Karen asked.

"Have you told me all your secrets? Norma and I shared a friendship that is hard to describe. She wrote a couple of times a month, and so did I. And we always talked on Sunday. We put things on paper that we'd never voice aloud to another person in the whole world."

Karen felt heat begin to creep up her neck and willed it to go away. No, she certainly had not told her mother all her secrets. She could scarcely face them herself, much less talk about them.

"Nanna, now what do we do?" Sue asked.

"Kim goes to work on the computer to see where this place stands financially. We'll unpack and plan supper. Tomorrow morning bright and early we gather the vegetables, set up the fruit stand, and take stock of the orchard."

Karen smiled. "Let's steam some of these green beans with green onions and bacon. That ought to help me fill out the hideous overalls you insisted I purchase. Besides, you don't cook. Never have—unless you've got another secret up your sleeve."

Hannah shook her finger at Karen. "Never had a need to cook, but I could learn if I wanted to. You and Sue can cook supper. I'm going to my room and unpack while Kim looks over that computer, and then the two of us are going to the fruit stand and have a look at it. Freezer will be in the garage right out the kitchen door. Better get something out to thaw or we'll be living on vegetables."

Hannah unpacked her things and hung them in the closet with Norma's clothing. The bottom drawer of the dresser was empty as if Norma had known her time was short and she'd gotten things ready for Hannah. The letters were on the top shelf of the closet in shoe boxes. Three of them to be exact, with big numbers on the ends: 44–65, 66–99, 2000–. She'd think about those later. Right there in the space of only a few square inches was Hannah Cosby Brewer's lifetime on paper. More than a diary, it was her dreams, sorrows, joys. Sixty-plus years that she'd either have to share with her girls or burn and forget.

She sat down at the sturdy oak desk and opened a drawer. A lined writing tablet caught her eye. She picked it up and flipped the slick cover back to find familiar handwriting and her name at the top.

June 5

Dear Hannah,

Starting a letter now. It's early morning in Oklahoma. The sun isn't even up yet. I'm thinking of that night we went out the bedroom window and hid in the cotton fields on a blanket. I told you about Ricky and how I intended to marry him even if my father died from the hissy fit when he found out. We laughed and came in just before dawn crawled back through the window. We had to fake sleep when Momma came to get us for breakfast. I know I've told you before that that summer was the one highlight of my life, especially after...oh, well, you know the story. More later today...

Only there hadn't been a later today for Norma. Before she could come back, she'd died. Hannah sighed and laid the tablet on the top of the desk. They'd been two kindred spirits. She shut the door softly and went to see what Kim had found on the computer. If the farm was in financial difficulty, it wouldn't be long.

The office looked like a converted coat closet. There was enough room for a small computer desk, a filing cabinet on each side of it, the chair, and Kim. Hannah went back to the living room and brought back a cane-bottomed chair. She sat down and watched as Kim typed in numbers and passwords until a screen popped up.

Kim held up a tablet just like the one Hannah had found. "I found this in the drawer. It's got account numbers, passwords, everything I need to access anything. This is the account at the bank in Tishomingo. Look at this."

Hannah peered over her shoulder. "Is that actual money that can be withdrawn or some kind of assets that would have to be sold?"

"Real money. CDs are in a different account, according to the stuff in this tablet. Here's what the household bills are." She pulled up another screen as she talked.

"Electricity and insurance on the houses and equipment," Kim said. "No water bills or payments?"

"She paid cash, and there're three wells on the property," Hannah said. "She never believed in credit cards or borrowing money. So there're no financial problems?"

"No, ma'am. This place is a virtual gold mine. Norma was a millionaire more than twice over," Kim exclaimed.

"She was a good businesswoman."

"What did she spend her money on? Oh, here's an account marked scholarship," Kim said.

"A good portion went to educate women, didn't it?" Hannah said.

Kim turned the screen around so Hannah could see. "Several scholarships each year to more than one university in Oklahoma. Anonymous, but she had the final say-so in them. Look at this list of names."

"I know. She wrote to me each year, agonizing over which high school senior should get the money. It was a full four-year ride if they kept up their grades. In the last thirty years, she's provided the money for several doctors, a couple of lawyers, and at least ten schoolteachers. She put her money where it would do a lot of good."

"She was quite a woman. I wish I could have met her," Kim said.

Hannah didn't answer. She should have brought them to Oklahoma years ago. Back when Jesse died, because the vow she made to him was fulfilled the day they buried him in Morgantown. When he'd come to Oklahoma to marry her, he'd made her promise she'd never come back again or talk about why she'd been brought there. However, there was no excuse for the past years, other than she hadn't wanted to share her friendship with anyone. She didn't want the girls to hear the stories and she didn't really trust even Norma not to tell the tale of what happened that week she spent with her or the rest of the story afterward.

"Sue is thawing a roast the size of an elephant's haunch in the microwave to put it in the oven for supper. Did you find out you've inherited a million dollars in past taxes and a chigger ranch?" Karen asked from the doorway.

"Hardly." Kim shut down the computer and spun around in the chair. "Norma was very wealthy, and now Nanna is even richer. Why didn't she tell you that she was going to do this?"

"Norma had her reasons," Hannah said.

"And I bet you know what they were." Sue's eyes twinkled. "Come on, Nanna, tell us."

"We'll be here all summer. If I tell it all tonight, what will be left to entertain us through the long evenings? I'm going to take a walk. Kim, you can come along with me now that we know the bills are all paid, and the tax folks aren't going to come take our new farm away from us. I want to look at the fruit stand."

"Nanna, it's hot." Kim moaned.

"Yes, it is, and exercise will do us both good."

"You're the boss." Kim sighed.

"Thank you. Humor an old woman. You never know what it might lead to."

"The day you are old has never dawned and never will, but I'll walk with you. Think it's safe to leave these two alone? They might fight." Kim pointed at her mother and grandmother.

Karen, at nearly sixty, could pass easily for forty with her slim figure and intense blue eyes. Sue, almost forty, was often mistaken for Kim's sister. She was shorter than Karen and a little heavier, with brown hair and brooding blue eyes. A few freckles danced across her nose, and she didn't even bother trying to cover them with makeup. When she pulled her hair back in a ponytail, she looked like a college girl instead of a schoolteacher.

"Leave two butcher knives on the bar. If they fight, they might as well make it 'unto death,' and we'll help the survivor bury the deceased when we get back," Hannah said.

"Nanna, that's gross." Kim shuddered.

"Then let's leave them to find their own weapons." Hannah was out the front door before Kim could do anything but follow her.

The fruit stand sat just far enough back off the road for trucks and cars to park in front of it. It was no more than the length of a football field from the house, with nothing but pasture and sky on the south side, big oak trees across the road, and more pasture dotted with trees on the north side.

They were standing inside the fruit stand when a pickup truck came to a stop, kicking up enough dust to make Kim sneeze three times in rapid succession.

"Nanna, we can't stay here all summer. I'll be dead, and it won't involve a butcher knife." Kim groaned.

"You'll toughen up," Hannah said. "Or you'll die, because your job after we pick the garden every day is going to be running this fruit stand."

"Nanna, I think you've really lost your marbles."

"For the first time in my life, I feel like I haven't lost anything. Like I'm right where I'm supposed to be. Like everything is in place now. Look! That's not a customer out there, disappointed that our fruit stand isn't opened up today. That's John!"

He leaned out the window. "Miz Hannah, what are you doing outside in the heat of the day? Need a ride back up to the house?"

Hannah said, "We're just about to turn around and go back. This heat is more pressing than we're used to in the mountains of West Virginia. You got supper plans?"

"I'm a gourmet cook." John grinned. "I make the best bologna sandwiches in Johnston County."

Hannah giggled. "Why don't you come around about six thirty for supper? That roast Sue put in the oven looked like it would feed an army."

"Thank you. I'd love to if it's not too much trouble. Could I bring Luke?" John said without hesitation.

"Yes, and it's no trouble. You'll be doing us a favor, actually. We've spent four days in the van together with no outside company. Kim's actually afraid her mother and grandmother might go at it with butcher knives while we're out for a walk."

"Then it'll be my duty," John said.

"We'll look for you then at six thirty," Kim said.

He drove away and Kim and Hannah turned and started back to the house.

"Did you plan that?" Kim asked. "Are you matchmaking?"

"Never been accused of such a thing. I figure women ought to do their own choosing, even if it's dead wrong. But your mother could use a little prodding, don't you think? And that John is a fairly handsome man. It's not like she's only interested in multimillionaires. She's a self-proclaimed antimaterialistic woman, and John's just a good old hardworking country boy."

"Nanna! You are matchmaking. Is that why you came out here?"

"Not me. I'm just inviting two men to supper so we can have some dinner conversation about gardens." Hannah winked.

CHAPTER FIVE

John and Luke arrived right on time. Sue opened the door to find them freshly shaven, wearing faded jeans and snowy white T-shirts, and holding their straw hats.

"Come right in," she said.

John's face was a study of angles ending with a square chin with just enough dimple in it to give him fits when he shaved. His green eyes were shot through with flecks of gold, and his salt-and-pepper hair had been combed straight back. His mouth was full and his smile honest.

"This is Luke, the rascal cowboy from south of you all. Luke, meet Hannah, Karen, Sue, and Kim," John said.

Luke hung his hat on one of the hooks behind the door. "Glad to meet y'all. We've heard your names often. But somehow I thought Kim was just a little girl, the way Norma always talked."

"Hardly," Kim said. "I'll be twenty this summer."

"I see that." His eyes started at her feet and traveled up to her dirty-blonde hair. He'd always been attracted to dark-haired girls. Blondes were far too delicate and ditzy for him.

She wanted to slap him for looking at her like she was trash. He didn't even know that she was pregnant, and he had no right to be so insolent anyway. She was married the night she conceived the baby.

Hannah sat down at one end of the small dining room table and motioned for John to sit at the other. "We might as well visit over supper. Karen and Kim on this side. Luke, you sit across from Kim and Sue on the end to John's left. That way she can get in and out to the kitchen easily to keep bowls refilled," she explained.

"So which of you ladies made this scrumptious meal?" John asked.

"Sue did," Hannah said. "Karen helped, but Sue is the cook. Karen has a full-time staff at her house. Sue does her own housework and cooking."

Karen passed the platter of roast beef to her mother. "She doesn't have to."

"But I choose to. Did Norma play the piano?" Sue changed the subject.

"No, never touched it 'cept to dust it every week. Kept it all pretty and shiny. Used to have a pool table in that corner. She could whip everyone in the whole county, I'm telling you. Sunday afternoons was pool time. We'd put on some country music and chalk up the cue sticks. She liked Alan Jackson, George Strait, Dolly Parton, and Loretta Lynn. Conway Twitty was a favorite too. Sometimes I could talk her into a little bit of Brad Paisley or Blake Shelton. Then one Saturday night we saw a big delivery truck from Dallas backing into the driveway. She sent the pool table over to John's. The piano went right there. Been about a year ago now," John said between bites.

"Kim plays," Hannah said.

Kim felt someone glaring at her and met Luke's cold gaze when she looked up. She met it without blinking until he looked down at his plate.

"So what do you play? Classical?" John asked.

"I took lessons for a couple of years when I was a little girl, but they wanted me to play classical. It's all right if you like it, but it didn't appeal to me one bit."

"What do you like?" Luke's blue eyes gave off a freeze even colder than the wind off a fresh West Virginia snow.

"Country, mostly. Floyd Kramer is my idol. I also like old gospel. Not the new stuff like alternative or gospel rock, but the things in the old, old hymn books. Please pass those green beans, Momma. They look wonderful." Kim avoided looking across the table again.

"At your age? You like country and gospel?" John asked.

"My dad's influence. His mother played a mean Floyd Kramer piano and she loved gospel music. She died last year, but I have the most fantastic memory of her fingers moving all over that piano. She taught me to love the tinkling sound of old gospel and country music. You know what the Good Book says: 'Raise up a child in the way he should go and he shall not depart from it.' She did her job well. I'm hoping that I run into Blake Shelton while we are here," Kim said.

"You might. I hear he goes to the Milburn bar every now and then and that he's just a regular person in Tishomingo," John told her.

Sue pushed her chair back and laid a plaid cloth napkin beside her plate. She picked up the tea pitcher and refilled John's glass, then Karen's and Hannah's and realized that Kim had water in her glass.

"Why aren't you having tea? You've always said a sit-down meal isn't a real dinner without sweet tea."

Kim held up a finger until she swallowed. "I'm on a new kick. No caffeine for a few weeks."

"Why?" Luke asked.

"I do this occasionally. Go on a kick to cleanse my aura or such," Kim answered. She knew she wasn't supposed to drink, and she could easily do without even a glass of wine, but she wouldn't know about caffeine until she had time to do some research. And that was not an easy feat with three older women around all the time.

"Sounds crazy to me. I'd die without tea, coffee, and Coke. When I'm a hundred years old and they do my autopsy, they'll find my blood is ninety percent caffeine," he said.

"What'll the other ten percent be?" Kim locked eyes with him but that time she didn't blink.

"Norma's strawberry jelly," John said. "He can eat a pint a week."

"Did she have recipes stored away?" Karen asked.

Luke nodded. "Her recipes must be somewhere in those cabinets. Which reminds me, the donkeys need feeding. Did you all do that yet?"

"After dishes. You know the rules," John told him.

"Yes, sir," Luke said.

"What rules?" Hannah asked.

John inhaled deeply. "I don't want you ladies to feel obligated but, when Norma was here..." He swallowed hard.

"Spit it out, son," Hannah said.

John nodded. "Friday night when the work week was finished we always ate at her house. It's kind of nice that you invited us since this is the first week without her, but we don't want you to think you have to keep up the traditions she started. Norma cooked and we did the cleanup. That was the rule. After supper, we played Monopoly or gin rummy or whatever she wanted. There's a Scrabble board here too. Then on Sunday, supper was at my place and we'd play pool. Rules say whoever cooks does not clean up. So we'll do the dishes tonight," John said.

"Then on Sunday you cook and we clean up?" Sue asked.

John blushed. "You wouldn't have to. It's just the way we did things when she was here."

"I like the rule. Are we invited, then, for dinner at your place on Sunday after church? We'll do the cleanup and I bet Kim can whip Luke at pool," Hannah said.

"Nanna!" Kim exclaimed.

"How much?" Luke's eyes narrowed.

She might be pretty, but he'd show her who was boss at the pool tables.

"Five bucks," Hannah said.

"You are on," Luke said.

"Now tell us about this garden business and the donkeys," Sue said. "Is it very big? And donkeys? What do they do?"

"Two full acres of garden, but that includes the strawberries," John said.

"Don't let him fool you. Six hundred and forty acres!" Luke chuckled. His eyes changed when he laughed. The veil lifted and they were downright dreamy.

Kim studied him in her peripheral vision. He was so handsome when he smiled that she was amazed that the clouds didn't part and a big booming voice didn't float out of heaven saying something wonderful. But when he looked at her again the veil was right back over his eyes.

"Really?" Karen exclaimed.

Surely they didn't have a garden that big, and if they did, 99 percent of it was about to wither up and die.

John laughed out loud. "No, he's trying to scare you ladies. Norma was a stickler about her garden. Part of it is strawberries, but they've already been harvested this year. She froze most of them, so you can play at making jam all you want to." He looked at Karen.

"Everything else is going strong. Matter of fact, the beans and zucchini need to be picked again, though. And there's yellow crookneck squash and cucumbers that'll go to waste if you don't bring them in," John explained.

"What did she do with zucchini?" Karen asked.

"Sold it in the stand, mostly. Some of it she made into pickles and sold. House smelled like sweet vinegar when she did that," John said.

"I'd love to try that," Karen said.

"Recipes for everything she made are under the bar. She said one time that they were passed down from her granny to her momma and then to her," John said. "Guess I'd better tell you the peaches will be ready pretty soon. She got enough to make a cobbler for us last Friday night, but when they start coming off you can hardly take care of them."

"What'd she use them for? Jams?" Karen asked.

"Jam, or she had this way of cannin' them so they was pretty in the jars, and she sold a whole bunch in the fruit stand," Luke said.

"I want to try my hand at making all of those things," Karen said.

John could have shouted. These women weren't such city slickers after all. He'd worried all week about whether they'd sweep in, take one look at the place, and put it on the market to sell. Miss Norma had painted a pretty picture of them all through the years, but he'd feared that she'd seen them through the rose-colored glasses of a teenaged girl.

"Then I guess we'll make pickles tomorrow. Does the zucchini just produce one time or does it produce all summer? We're not too smart when it comes to gardening, but we're fast learners," Sue asked.

"Oh, you'll be sick of it by the time fall comes," Luke said. "Norma said she saw the green squash in her sleep at night and the vines tried to strangle her, but she never wasted a single one of them."

He'd admit it when he was wrong. But before he admitted anything, he had to be absolutely sure he'd been wrong!

Women interested in making pretty jelly and jams and pickles didn't make him wrong. He'd hold his judgment until they broke their backs picking tomatoes and zucchini. And when one of them endured that hot fruit stand for hours and days on end.

CHAPTER SIX

Karen slipped into a white cotton sundress with spaghetti straps and a huge hand-painted rose on the circular skirt. She added a red bolero jacket and a pair of Italian leather sandals. She was the first one in the kitchen that Sunday morning, so she made coffee, and then made cinnamon toast from the rest of a loaf of bread Sue had baked the day before.

Hannah was ready long before Karen, but she spent a few extra minutes in Norma's room. Norma's spirit hadn't left the house yet. It wasn't a bad thing, and Hannah had an idea after the talk around the table during supper and the Scrabble game about why. She just had to wrap her thinking around the concept that Norma had had a forewarning about her death and got things ready for them in her own way.

"What is it you want me to do?" She whispered.

A quiet voice in her heart said simply, *Not one thing. You've already done it.*

Hannah smiled, understanding a little more. "Guess we both kept at least one secret, didn't we, Norma? It could work. I could push the idea a little if worse comes to worst."

Kim finished dressing in a long broomstick skirt, each tier a shade of brown with turquoise sequins dotting it here and there, and a sleeveless ecru-colored cotton sweater. She picked up her shoes, nothing more than straps across her arch and behind her heel, with laces that crisscrossed halfway to her knees. Securing her long hair into a ponytail at the nape of her neck, she hoped the preacher didn't sermonize about keeping secrets before God and feeling guilty about it.

For the first time the Brewer women were bonding, and she could not destroy the fragile cord. Maybe by the time she could say the word *pregnant* aloud again and tell them the story about Marshall, the news wouldn't snap the thin rope.

Sue wore a bright orange linen sheath that barely touched her knees and a pair of high-heeled sandals. She barely took time to check her makeup. Her thoughts went to the dozen quarts of zucchini pickles she'd helped Karen make the day before for the fruit stand. She'd have to share the recipe with her teacher friend when they all returned to West Virginia in the fall.

A feeling that she didn't like hit her, and she sat down with a thud on the white wrought-iron vanity bench.

"Nanna isn't going home. She's staying here. What went on that summer to draw her back to this place? I'm crazy. Of course she's going home. This place is nothing but dirt and sky and hard work, and I know that after only one day in the garden."

Kim opened the door and peeked inside. "Momma, you ready? Who are you talking to? You look like you just saw a ghost."

"I think I did, but I've been wrong before," Sue said. "Let's go to church. I can't remember a time when we all went together."

"It's because it never happened. Nanna watched services on television because she couldn't leave the hotel. I don't think Grandma has been in a church since she got married," Kim said.

"Oh, yes, she has. She drug me to Sunday morning services my whole life. At least until that summer when she went to Italy. Something changed her, because we didn't go after that. Not that I minded back then," Sue said honestly.

The doorbell sent them to the front of the house to find John and Luke in the foyer. Hannah and Karen were picking up their purses and heading for the door.

Sue's breath caught in her chest. John was dressed in a shirt with white pearl snaps, black creased western-cut slacks that hugged his muscular thighs, and black eel cowboy boots.

"We're used to coming by to pick up Norma," John explained. "We hadn't talked about whether you'd be attending this morning or not, but we could show you the way. Don't have room in the truck to haul everyone, or we could all go together, but we'll be glad to show you where our pew is. It's our first Sunday without her."

"We'll follow you," Hannah said.

Kim was speechless. Luke looked like he'd just walked out of a commercial for cowboy boots. He held a black Stetson hat in his hands; his blond hair was feathered back perfectly. His slacks fit like they'd been tailored just for him and a tooled belt with an engraved silver belt buckle was laced through the wide loops. His black cowboy boots were polished to a shine so high that she could see the reflection of her skirt tail in them.

John offered his arm to Hannah, who looped hers through it and allowed him to lead her out to the van. He opened the passenger door and helped her inside.

"You ladies look lovely today," he said.

"Thank you," Sue said. "You two don't look so shabby yourselves."

John chuckled. "That sounds like Norma. Last Sunday she said we cleaned up fairly well for two old Okie farmers."

The church parking lot was full with less than a dozen cars lined up right in front of the front door. John pulled into the lot for the Milburn Family Clinic, right across the street to the south, and Sue nosed her van in beside him. The men were out and opening the doors for them before Sue could put the keys in her purse.

"Thank you." Hannah smiled.

"Usually it's not so full, but since Norma didn't want a funeral, I expect the congregation is expecting the preacher to make up for it today. And these folks don't mind if we use their lot on days when the church is full." John offered his arm to Hannah again. Karen and Sue fell in behind them, with Luke and Kim bringing up the rear.

"Oh, dear. We aren't dressed for a memorial service," Sue whispered to Hannah.

"Norma would have told you that you are all beautiful and she would have been right," John told her.

They entered the church and the whole congregation stood as if it were a funeral. John and Hannah led the tiny procession to the front, where John stepped back to let Hannah go to the far end of the pew with Karen right behind her. Sue followed her and John stepped ahead of Luke and went in to sit beside Sue, leaving Luke to sit beside Kim.

The preacher made a motion with his arms and there was a shuffling as everyone sat back down and reached for the hymnals on the backs of the pews.

"Our friend Norma left our presence last Monday. The letter she left for me said there was to be no funeral and she was to be cremated, but that the first Sunday after Hannah and her girls arrived we could have a memorial service. Today we will have a celebration of life for our dear friend and a pillar in our society. Our pianist is sick with the flu today, but we understand Kim DeHaven, the great-granddaughter of Miss Norma's relative, Hannah Brewer, can play, so we're going to ask her to help us out as we sing some of Miss Norma's favorite hymns."

Kim wanted to shoot Luke. He didn't have to tell that she could play, and it had to be his fault. No doubt, the preacher had called to tell him that there couldn't be music that morning since their pianist was ill, and he'd tattled. There was nothing to do but stand to her feet and make her way past John and Luke, who were standing reverently, their hats on their hearts, but she did shoot him a look meant to fry him right there in front of the preacher and God.

The preacher smiled as she sat down on the piano bench. "Thank you, Kim. It would have meant a lot to Norma to have you play this morning. She talked of all you every time I visited with her. In the back of the hymnals you'll find a few sheets of music with her favorite songs. We thought you'd like to take them with you to remember her by, since there are no memorial folders. Kim, if you are ready, we'll sing, 'When We All Get to Heaven,' and sing it from your hearts, loud enough to ring in the courts of heaven, where Miss Norma can hear you. You know she wasn't one to mince words or sing like a bird. When she sang, she opened her heart and let it ring."

Kim's fingers danced across the old upright piano as the church filled with the whole congregation singing, "I'll Fly Away," and then "Leaning on the Everlasting Arms."

The preacher said a few words about Norma, telling how long she'd been a part of the community and the church, but Hannah remembered a Sunday morning years before when she and her mother had attended church with Norma and her family. Ricky had sat behind them and kept toying with Norma's long hair. Her father would have skinned him alive and tacked his skin to the smokehouse door if he'd known.

The preacher nodded toward a young woman sitting on the front pew and said, "Norma gave me a tape a few weeks ago. It's got one song on it and she said I was to play it the Sunday after she died if Hannah Brewer was here. If not, I was to send the tape to her by mail. Alan Jackson is the singer, and the song is 'I Want to Stroll Over Heaven With You.' When this song is finished, services are over for today. We lost a great lady. I'm glad those who loved her are here with us today."

The woman smiled at Kim, still sitting at the piano in case there were more songs she needed to play, and put the tape in a recorder on the top of the piano.

Hannah had done well until Alan Jackson's voice filled the church. He talked about all the good things that came from above and all the blessings, and how he'd ask a favor from the King. Tears began to flow down her cheeks when he sang about places, time, and treasure keeping them from making plans while they were on Earth but that there would come a day when they would stroll over heaven together. By the time it ended, Luke had given her his handkerchief and it was wet with tears.

Yes, my dear friend, we will take that stroll. We'll leave all the heartaches and troubles behind and we'll stroll through the streets and laugh and talk for all eternity. Find a bench and wait for me. I won't be long. Just a few short months.

She was still sniffling when they reached home.

Home. A strange word, she thought, but she was home and she wasn't leaving. Karen, Sue, and even Kim would throw a fit, but John and Luke could take care of her just like they did Norma. In the summers her girls could come home and help with the garden and fruit stand, and they'd all have a fine time together. She'd look forward to it all year.

You'll be strolling over heaven with Norma before another summer and you know it, so don't be making long-range plans.

"That was lovely," Karen said. "So much better than a somber old funeral. I'm glad none of us knew and that we didn't wear black suits."

"Yes, it was." Hannah sighed.

"Good grief," Kim said.

"What?" Sue asked.

"There's a whole line of cars and trucks coming up the road and they're turning in here."

Hannah smiled. "Funeral dinner, whether she likes it or not."

"What?" Sue asked again.

"Wait and see," Hannah said.

The first woman to knock on the door was about Hannah's age. "Hannah, I know what Norma wanted, but we've come to set up dinner in the backyard under the pecan trees. We brought everything we need, so y'all just come on out here and get acquainted with the community. Person ought to know their neighbors. I'm Edith and we met once when you was just a girl and come out here to visit Norma."

"Thank you," Hannah said. "I remember you. Y'all lived in the town of Emet."

Edith looped her arm into Hannah's and led her out to the yard. "Still do, darlin', and we're glad you've come to hold the farm down. Now you just take a seat in one of them chairs the men folks is unfolding and we'll have a visit while the young folks get this food on the tables."

"And what was your maiden name?" Hannah asked.

"I was Edith Lockhart back before I married the first time. Met you the summer of 1944 when you came out here to visit Norma. This is Myrtle Long and this is Virgie Perdew. Ladies, this here is Hannah Brewer, Norma's cousin. They haven't lived here since the sixth day of creation, so they wouldn't remember how things were back then. But they did know Norma and her folks the past fifty years anyway."

Karen and Sue set about helping the middle-aged women put dozens of covered dishes on the tables. Kim filled plastic cups with ice and set them on a card table beside the five-gallon container of sweet tea.

Hannah put names with faces.

Edith had thick gray chin-length hair, soft blue eyes, and twice as many wrinkles as Hannah. Myrtle had a little pepper left in her wispy short salty-gray hair. She was short, thin and wore a denim skirt with a chambray shirt. Virgie's hair was stovepipe black, right out of a Miss Clairol bottle, and ratted up into a 1960s beehive look. She wore a white peasant blouse with a big ruffle around the neck and a sweeping skirt with enormous red roses on a black background.

"Could I get you some tea, Miz Hannah?" Luke asked.

"Yes, and did you know about this?" Hannah asked.

"Yes, ma'am, but I didn't want to spoil the surprise," Luke said.

Kim turned around to fill a glass with ice and ran right into Luke. It felt like she'd hit an oak tree when she put her hands on his chest to break her fall. His arms automatically grabbed for her and held her tightly until she got her bearings.

"You trying to knock me down and break my arm so you don't have to shoot eight ball with me later?" he asked.

She took a step back. "Are you trying to addle me so that I won't beat you? I could whip you with one hand tied behind me and a patch over one eye."

Luke looked down his nose at her. "Maybe in your dreams, Miss Fancy Pants."

She poked a finger in his broad chest. "Don't call me names, Mr. Smart Aleck. You don't know jack about me."

"And I don't care to know anything about you, lady. See you at dinner tonight. Leave your patch at home. You'll need all the skill you can muster to whip me." Luke poured a plastic glass full of tea and carried it to Hannah.

An elderly man stopped by Hannah's chair. "Sorry to hear about Norma. Seems strange for her to be gone. I always figured she would be around forever. In my mind she was ten feet tall and bulletproof. I live across the road and down a piece. Y'all need anything, you just call me. I'm Rupert O'Dell and I'm in the book."

"Thank you. I'll miss her. She was my best friend, even though I didn't ever come back after that one visit. We kept in touch by mail," Hannah said.

"Yes, ma'am, we all knew that," he said and moved on.

"And lots of phone calls, I'd bet," Edith said.

"Every Sunday," Hannah said.

"So did it come as a surprise for Norma to leave you the farm?" Edith asked.

"Yes, it did," Hannah said.

"I told these girls it would. Everyone expected John or Luke to get it. John's been like a grandson, and Luke, well, he's lived next door to her his whole life. Guess she's got her reasons, though. At our age, we don't know as much as we did when we was sixteen like we did that summer, do we?" Edith laughed.

"What happened that summer y'all are talking about? And did you see the way Luke and the youngest of your tribe was acting? They looked like they were fixin' to have it out right there at the tea table," Myrtle said.

"Ain't that sweet. Fight first, kiss later is what I say," Virgie said.

Hannah glanced that way and smiled.

Norma, were you going for a double shot? Well, good luck with that one. I don't see it happening.

"Hey, I remember that summer when you were here. That was the summer Norma's daddy found out Norma was in love with Ricky and sent him packing," Edith said, and the subject went back to Norma and Ricky.

"Good Lord, Norma and the hired help? I guess that about put him into a tailspin. I remember him well, and he was staid right up until the day he died."

"Times were different then," Hannah said. "Men were losing their power, so they were clutching at it like it was their lifeline. My daddy was the same way. His word was the law and no one dared disobey it."

"Strange, ain't it, the way things changed? Norma was just born a couple of generations too early. Nowadays, nobody pays any attention to those kinds of things or to race," Edith said.

"The hired hand was a Mexican?" Virgie asked. "Good Lord, I remember one time when I was a girl, I got a bad crush on one of the cotton pickers who was from Mexico. Daddy almost shipped me off to a boarding school in Boston because of it. Mother kept me tied so close to her apron strings until the cotton was all picked that there wasn't no way I could even speak to the boy again. Never saw him after that summer and that's been sixty-four years ago. Tell you the truth, though, I still get the flutters when I picture him in my mind."

"Happens that way sometimes." Hannah nodded.

"So when are y'all going back to the east? Staying all summer, or you going back once you get things straightened out? Going to sell the place to John?" Edith asked.

"No, we're staying. Kind of liked the place once we got here. My daughter, Karen, is dying to try her hand at making jellies, jams, and pickles. The way she dives into a business, she'll have a factory going around here." Hannah smiled.

She lowered her voice and said, "She's also in the middle of a messy divorce and needs a change of scenery. My granddaughter, Sue, is a schoolteacher, but she's agreed to learn how to garden. She's already finding out she's a natural at it, and she's a good cook, so she's been taking care of the harvest out of the garden. And no, we aren't selling the place. We'll be keeping it in the family." Hannah sipped her coffee.

"What about that young one? The one who played the piano at the church? Think she'd be interested in taking over my job?" Myrtle asked. "My old hands have gotten arthritis so bad it's painful for me to play on Sunday, but there hasn't been nobody else who'd take the job."

"Sure, she will do it." Hannah nodded.

"Reckon you better ask her first?" Virgie asked.

"She'll do it," Hannah said.

"Hey, did y'all hear that Gracie Wiggins is in the hospital? I told that woman last summer if she didn't throw away that old walker and get herself back on her feet she'd be dead in a year," Myrtle said, changing the subject.

"Gracie was old when she was forty-five. She's been dying for years of acute hypochondria." Edith giggled.

"Ain't it the truth. Every time I run into her she talks about cancer or ulcers. Maybe she finally got one or the other. Guess we'd best make plans to go see her tomorrow," Virgie said.

"Ya'll still drive, then?" Hannah asked.

"Sure we do. Lord, I'm careful about keeping my license up-to-date more than I worry about the taxes on the property. They'll send me a notice if my taxes are overdue. If they cut off my driver's license then I'd be up crap creek without a paddle. There ain't no way I could pass that test. When I got my license, I just went down to the drugstore and bought it. Wasn't no test in them days. Just lay out your money and they give you a license," Virgie said.

"Well, then, come out anytime. We can sit around in my kitchen and have coffee and you can visit with my girls," Hannah said.

"Thank you," they chimed in together, two gray heads and one coal-black nodding in unison.

John raised his voice and held up a hand. "Could I have a moment? Hannah and her family and Luke and I would like to thank everyone for this meal today. Norma would have liked this. She always looked forward to my summer barbecue for the community, so I know she would have loved this day, especially since Hannah and her family are here. I'm going to ask our preacher to say grace and then we'll let

Hannah lead the line through the buffet. If you'll bow your heads with me…"

The preacher blessed the food and the minute he said, "Amen," the noise started again. Hannah and her new friends Edith, Virgie, and Myrtle led the line past the tables and settled back in their chairs to gossip some more.

By midafternoon the backyard was cleaned up and the company all gone. Hannah sat in the middle rocking chair on the porch and looked out over her land. She couldn't remember the last time she'd gossiped with women her age or made friends in a single afternoon. As acting queen of the hotel, she graced the dining room with her presence each evening, but the guests were acquaintances. They were people you asked about their lives and the answer was given in one-syllable words like "fine." They never used words like *cancer* and *ulcers* in their answers.

❖ ❖ ❖

Kim slumped down into the chair beside her. "Nanna, I've never seen anything like that in my whole life."

"It's small-town living. If we'd been here the day of her death, they would have brought food in by the bushels," Nanna said.

Karen sat down in the other chair. "They did today. Does this happen every time someone dies?"

Hannah nodded. "Or gets sick or goes to the hospital. It's just the way it is."

"Well, I like it," Sue said.

Hannah's face hurt from smiling all day and not a single one of them had been fake. "Me too. Let's go inside and take a nap. We've got about an hour before we need to drive over to John's house. I believe I've got five dollars on a pool game, and if you let me down Norma is liable to sit on my bedpost and haunt me tonight."

❖ ❖ ❖

John wrapped potatoes in foil and tossed them in the oven. A salad of fresh endive, tomatoes, homemade garlic croutons, and a spicy southwestern dressing he whipped up himself chilled in the refrigerator along with sliced and sugared strawberries for shortcake. He grilled steaks that had marinated all night in special sauce. Luke made corn on the cob and fried yellow squash. The table was set for six in his country kitchen.

The van pulled up and he slung open the door before they had time to knock. "Come right on in. Luke has been frothing at the bit to heat up the pool table before dinner. Tea for everyone?"

"Yes, sir," Kim said.

"Did you get that precious aura cleansed?" Luke asked.

"Yes, I did. Now I'm on tea part of the time and fresh lemonade the rest. I'm laying off carbonated drinks because I understand they hinder the eyesight and I'm going to whip you soundly at the pool table this evening," she taunted.

"You bring your eye patch?" Luke asked.

"You got a bandanna? You can tie it around my head and uncover one eye," she smarted off.

Luke finally smiled. "I'll take your five-dollar bill without hobbling you."

"Bring it on, big boy!" Kim said.

It wasn't even a close game. Luke broke the balls and failed to put the first one in the pocket. From there, Kim was in control and he never used his cue stick again.

"Beginner's luck." He slapped another five on the edge of the table.

"Boy, either you are a sucker or you like to give away money," she taunted.

He racked up the balls and stood back. "Go ahead."

She put three in the pockets and missed.

He put two in and missed the third one.

From there he stood to one side and she ran the table on him the second time.

"Where did you learn to play like that?"

"Voodoo." She laughed.

Luke nodded. "I believe it. I think you could will those balls into the pockets and how come my cue stick is made of wood and yours of bendable rubber?"

"Voodoo," she said again, waving her hands in the air like a snake charmer.

Sue patted him on the shoulder. "Her father was a champion pool player. He played in tournaments and taught her to play before she cut her teeth. Lots of times when we were down to our last dollar, he'd take her to the pool hall and come home with twenty, and that would last us until payday. Your money was gone before you got it out of your pocket and Nanna knew it. One time Kim won five hundred dollars in a single evening in a pool hall in Morgantown, but the stakes were higher than five dollars a game."

"Momma, how did you know that?"

"Morgantown might have eighty thousand people, but honey, you couldn't drive to the mall without me knowing how fast you were going, where you stopped for a Coke, and how many friends you had in the car with you. I keep telling you I've got radar in my brains. Mommas get them the day they have a child or adopt one."

"And they never lose them," Hannah said.

"Oh, and how much do you know about me?" Karen joked.

"I'm eighty years old. What do you want me to remember or forget?" Hannah asked.

Karen blushed.

"Well, I'm not saying a word," Sue tried to joke, but inside she wondered if her mother had the slightest inkling of all she'd gotten involved in during her teenage years.

"Time to slap the steaks on the grill for supper. How do y'all like yours?" John asked.

"Medium is fine with me," Kim said.

"I think the rest of us eat ours the same way," Hannah said.

"That's right." Sue nodded along with Karen.

"Wipe the slobbers from his face, skin him, and slap him on the grill for five minutes on each side," Luke said.

"*Cowboy Way*. You don't get to claim that line as your own. Pepper said it in the movie," Kim said.

Luke was shocked. "You watch old westerns."

Kim nodded.

John clapped him on the shoulder. "Guess you've met your match."

Luke narrowed his eyes. "Drive a tractor?"

"Of course. You think we plow with mules in Virginia? Grandma DeHaven has a garden and I plow it for her every year."

Sue opened her mouth to say that the tractor looked more like a riding lawnmower and the garden was about the size of Norma's patio, but she clamped it shut. Kim could fight her own battles and Luke had best watch his back.

After supper, Hannah yawned. "I'm sorry. It's just been a big day and I'm exhausted. Would it be too rude if Karen and I went on home? I'll leave Sue and Kim to do the cleanup."

"Not tonight. Luke and I'll take care of it. We used paper plates, so there's nothing much to do anyway," John said.

"You sure?" Sue asked. "We don't mind."

John waved her away with his hand. "Not a bit. And the recipe for the marinade on the steaks is in Norma's cookbook. She taught me how to make it."

"I'll whip you by the end of the summer," Luke yelled at Kim as she was leaving.

"You better practice long and hard," Kim shot over her shoulder.

She got into the backseat with Hannah and hummed the song Alan Jackson had sung all the way down the lane to their house. *Their house.* Now where did that idea come from? They'd been in Oklahoma only two days and already she thought of Norma's as *their house*? How weird was that? True, in the week since they'd left Morgantown they'd formed a bond that sure enough hadn't been there before, but she could melt that glue with two words: *I'm pregnant.*

Hannah went straight to her room and kicked her shoes off. She stretched out on the bed, wiggling her toes and letting her thoughts meander.

Karen moved the coffee table and tossed the rug aside. She curled up on the sofa in the cellar with Norma's canning book in her hand. Tomorrow, after they'd harvested the garden for the day, she intended to try her hand at strawberry jam.

Sue picked up a fat romance novel and kicked back in a recliner. The cowboy hero looked like John. If the heroine had looked like her, she might have fantasized for a minute or two, but the lady was a red-haired vixen with violet eyes and lips made for kissing. She sighed, opened the book, and fell asleep before she finished the first page.

Kim sat down in one of the rocking chairs on the porch and watched the sun set. Friday, they had arrived. Saturday, they'd harvested and organized the produce for the fruit stand the next day. Sunday had been an experience all day long. Tomorrow, she'd be up and selling produce by eight o'clock.

A week ago, she hadn't even known she was pregnant, and now her world was bigger in some ways and so much smaller in others. Which one did she like best? Which one would she wind up living in?

CHAPTER SEVEN

"There's not much to explain," the lawyer said. "First thing I need you to do is identify the people in this picture." He laid a black-and-white photograph in front of Hannah. The other three women drew closer to see.

Hannah picked up a pair of reading glasses from beside her coffee cup and set them on her nose. "That would be Norma's mother, then my mother, me, and Norma, and that is Ricky. Her father took the picture. He didn't want Ricky in the photo, but Norma insisted. There would be another one of Norma's mom and dad, me, and my mother without Ricky. Can I keep this picture?"

"Yes, it's yours. And what was Ricky's full name?"

"Rodrique Luiz Encio," Hannah said. "Ricky was his nickname. Why did you need to know who these people are?"

"Norma said an impostor could identify everyone but Ricky, and only you would remember his full name. She said it was her insurance policy that no fake Hannah would come sniffing around wanting a farm. The rest of it is cut and dried, just like John told you. All I need are a few signatures stating you are accepting the inheritance."

Hannah adjusted her reading glasses on the end of her nose, tipped her head just right, and began to read the papers he put in front of her. When she finished, she signed her name.

She laid her glasses to one side and said, "I need you to draw up a simple will."

Tillman took a yellow legal pad and sharpened pencil from his briefcase.

"Mother, you have a will with our lawyers back home," Karen said.

Hannah nodded seriously. "Yes, I do, and that will be changing soon too. But this will is to take care of this property, not the hotel. Please draw one up that says when I die everything Norma has left me will be divided equally among these three women, as long as one of them lives on the property and oversees the farm and keeps the fruit stand open in the summer. They can all live here or they can come and go, but someone must be in residence here at all times," Hannah said.

"Nanna!" Kim exclaimed.

Hannah held up a hand. "That's easy enough, isn't it?"

The lawyer nodded and put his paper and pencil away. "I can have this done by the end of the week. Want me to bring it back out here for you to sign?"

"No, I'll come into town on Friday and take care of it then."

"Then good day to you ladies. I always liked Norma and if I can be of help to you then call. I'm semiretired, but I take care of my neighbors and friends here in Emet." Tillman snapped his worn briefcase shut and headed toward the door.

"Thank you," Hannah said.

When he was gone, Hannah looked around the table at four sober faces. "I'm not leaving this place until I die and I want to know one of you will be here to keep my spirit happy."

"Mother! You're not going home?" Karen gasped.

So I was right, Sue thought.

"No, I'm not going back to Morgantown. I am home, Karen," Hannah said.

Kim studied the picture. "Gosh, Nanna, I look a lot like you."

"Yes, you do. Now let's talk seriously. I knew when I left the hotel I wasn't going back."

"Why?" Sue asked.

"Because I like it here. I've got you three around me every day. It's an old woman's dream," Hannah said.

"But, Nanna, we'll go home at the end of the summer and you'll be here all alone," Kim said.

"Let's talk seriously about that. Karen, are you planning on going back to the winery in Morgantown or did you find something down in the cellar to interest you?" Hannah asked bluntly.

"Of course I'll go home. Daniel and I will run the business together like we always have," Karen said.

"What would you do if you could do anything?" Hannah asked. "Answer me honestly."

Karen inhaled. "Honestly? I'd sell the Brewer Winery to Daniel. All of it. Label, house, and all. I'd start my own label on a brand-new venture into specialty jams, jellies, and pickles. I even found a recipe in those books for pickled watermelon rind and pickled peaches. I bet you can't find that anywhere in a market. I'm sixty years old in less than a month. Is that too old to start all over?"

"You won't be any younger next year," Kim said.

"You don't think I'm crazy?" Karen smiled.

Kim shook her head. "No, I don't."

"Well, thank you for your vote of confidence," she said. "I'll think about it through the summer. I'll even try my hand at making it and see where it goes."

"Follow your heart and there will be peace," Kim said.

"Out of the mouths of babes." Hannah smiled.

Kim looked at Sue. "Now, Momma, what about you? If Grandma goes back, would you be willing to live on this farm to inherit it?"

Sue shrugged. "I don't know. I like it here. I've loved being with you and having Mother and Nanna close, but I'm a teacher and my job is in Morgantown."

"I've been into the financials on this place. Money isn't a factor, Momma. You don't need to work at anything else but this farm. You hum when you are picking vegetables and working out in the dirt. I haven't heard you hum since Daddy died," Kim said.

"I'm almost forty. I don't make rash decisions anymore and just because I like to be outside and hum doesn't mean I'm going to do something stupid. I'd have to think about it too," she said.

Hannah stood up. "We'll give it to the end of summer, then. Edith called yesterday to see if I was going to be home this morning and said they'd be by about eight. I'm going to make a pot of coffee and get out that lemon cake you made yesterday, Sue."

"You didn't ask me, Nanna," Kim said from the other side of the table.

"I don't have to ask you. If they both leave and go to Morgantown, you'll stay with me and inherit the whole she-bang when I'm gone," Hannah said.

"What makes you think that?" Sue said. "Kim's friends are in the east. This is nothing but hard work and dirt. You can't make the decision for her."

"Kim?" Hannah asked.

"I'm pregnant," she blurted out. "And I don't want to ever go back to Morgantown again."

Hannah's head jerked around to stare at Kim. "Well, there you have it. I've got one who'll stay with me. You are what?"

All the color drained from Sue's face. "Did you say you are pregnant?"

"She didn't stutter," Karen said. "When's the wedding?"

High color filled Kim's cheeks. "The wedding already happened and is over. We had it annulled."

Hannah patted her on the shoulder. "Lots of single mothers do just fine."

"Who is the father?" Sue gasped.

"Marshall Neville. He dated a girl all through high school and the first two years we were in college and they broke up. We met and dated, got married in Vegas over spring break, and then realized we'd made a big mistake, so his dad helped us annul it quietly. He has no idea about this baby. I don't intend to tell him, because he's marrying his old girlfriend in December."

"When?" Sue whispered.

"I just said he's getting married in December. Oh, you meant me, didn't you? Due February twenty-fifth," Kim said. "I just found out the morning we left Morgantown. Did one of those home tests. Haven't been to the doctor."

Hannah threw her arm around Kim's shoulders. "You can run a farm with a baby underfoot and there's plenty of room in the fruit stand for a baby. And I don't think I've even heard one of you sneeze since the first day, so you aren't allergic to Oklahoma."

"Nanna, I'll be twenty in August. How am I going to run an operation like this?"

"I ran a hotel when I was twenty and Karen was a baby. You're smarter than I was. I have faith in you," Hannah said.

Tears streamed down Kim's face. "I don't deserve your faith. I've ruined the family name."

Hannah laughed. Not a giggle, but a true laugh from the bottom of her chest. She wiped tears on the back of her hand and kept roaring as she wrapped her arm around Kim and hugged her tightly, nearly dragging her off the chair.

"Honey, you are pregnant. So what? If you think the Brewer name is spotless, then you are wrong. Now dry up those tears. This isn't going to stop the sun from coming up in the east every single day. I doubt if it even makes the evening news."

"I can't believe you just told her that." Karen gasped.

Hannah shook her finger at Karen. "Look on the bright side. Just think of the look on Tiffany's face when you tell her she's going to be a great-grandmother."

"Well, now, that does present a funny picture." Karen smiled.

Sue threw up her hands. "You are all crazy! This is not funny."

"Lighten up, Momma. If Nanna isn't going to crucify me, then you don't get to either," Kim said.

Sue's eyes flashed. "You are not old enough to have a child."

Kim pointed at Hannah. "Nanna was twenty when Grandma was born. She was that age when you were born and you were about the same age when I was born. I can raise this baby on my own and run this farm while I do it.

Nanna said so and her word is the law. I come from good stock, right, Nanna?"

Hannah nodded. "Way I see it, Sue, is that you aren't about to move away from your grandchild. So now I've got two of you in my pocket. The only one I have to win over is my own offspring, and she's going to be so busy making fancy stuff that by fall that she'll forget to go back east."

Kim reached across the table and laid her hand on Sue's. "I know this is hard for you, Momma. You've always been so perfect. I'm sorry I disappointed you."

Hannah cleared her throat. "Honey, I hate to break your bubble, but we are not perfect women. At least I'm not. Someday I'll tell you a story to back up that statement. It's time to open the fruit stand, so Kim needs to get out of here and get busy. You other two have pickles to make and canning to do. And I've got to get all this stuff you picked this morning organized and into baskets to take down to the fruit stand so we won't run out of produce by midmorning."

Sue looked out the window. "What's John doing here?"

Kim threw a hand over her mouth. "Oops!"

"What?" she asked.

"He called last evening on the house phone. Said that there's beehives on the back of the property and it's time to rob them. I was supposed to tell you and I forgot when we got busy with that squash relish last night. You are going with him, Momma, to learn how to get the honey away from the bees."

Sue shook her finger at Kim. "I don't know anything about bees."

"Well, Nanna has friends coming this morning. I have a fruit stand to run and Grandma already has the jars ready to make more squash relish. Who are we going to send? Go learn what it takes to make honey, get some in jars, and bring it to the stand. Several people asked me about it yesterday, so they'll be back today expecting to buy."

John rapped on the door and stuck his head inside. "Ready to rob the bees?"

"Yes, she is," Kim said.

Hannah bit the inside of her lip to keep from grinning.

❖ ❖ ❖

"What was that all about? Were y'all having a disagreement?" John opened the truck door for her.

Sue shivered when his arm brushed against hers. It wasn't fair to be attracted to a man she'd known less than two weeks. How in the devil did her life get so complicated in such a short time?

"Nanna is declaring that she's selling her hotel and living here permanently. She's going to leave this place to us, but one or all of us have to be in residence. I know what she's doing. She wants one of her own around all the time until she dies."

"Is that a bad thing? Norma dropped dead without anyone. I will always feel bad about that."

She cocked her head to one side and looked at him. "We've left lifelong friends and roots in West Virginia."

John drove down a lane with grass growing up between the tire tracks. "Life is not perfect, huh?"

"Far from it. Sometimes it's a big old mess," Sue said.

"Maybe it's a blessing in disguise."

"Do you always see the silver lining?" she asked.

He tapped the brakes and came to a stop. "The hives are a ways back there where it's nice and quiet. We'll carry our netting until we get there, unless you think you're a bee charmer. And yes, I try to see the silver lining."

"I'm not a bee charmer. I'm terrified of getting stung."

John chuckled and looked across the pickup seat. "You're pretty honest, aren't you?"

"Yes, I am."

He reached across the seat and laid a hand on hers. "Don't be afraid. Of the bees or of change. Hannah knows what she's doing. She's like Norma. Trust her. It will work out for the best."

She bit her lip to keep from gasping. "That's a lot of trust."

He removed his hand and rushed around the truck to open the door for her. "Yes, it is. Now let's get you all geared up to steal honey, honey!"

"That's a corny line, John Rayford."

He chuckled. "It is, isn't it, but I couldn't resist."

❖ ❖ ❖

Kim didn't even get to sit down before a car stopped and an elderly man bought okra, tomatoes, and green beans. She'd barely finished giving him change when a white pickup stopped and she looked up to see Luke standing right in front of the stand.

"I'll have a jar of that strawberry jam. Ate the last of mine for breakfast this morning," he said.

She picked up a jar and handed it to him. Their fingertips brushed and sparks danced around the fruit stand. He jerked his hand back and laid a bill on the counter.

"You aren't raisin' prices, are you?" he asked hoarsely.

"Not this year. Nanna says that things stay the same."

"Good!"

He drove away without looking back.

"What was that all about?" she asked but didn't have time to think about an answer. Two cars stopped and business went on.

❖ ❖ ❖

"Hey, Hannah!" Edith yelled from the back door.

Hannah motioned the three women inside.

"You sortin'?" Myrtle asked.

"That's my job."

"We'll help for a cup of coffee and something sweet. Even store-bought cookies will work fine." Virgie went to the sink, ran it full of water, and started washing the dirt from the zucchini.

"Sue made a lemon cake," Hannah said.

"That's even better."

Myrtle sat down at the table and started helping Hannah.

Edith went to the stove and looked inside the pot Karen was stirring. "Squash relish?"

Karen nodded.

Edith picked up a four-sided hand grater. "You been usin' this?"

"Yes, ma'am."

Edith opened the garage door and came back carrying a food processor. "This will make the job go faster. I'll grate and get things ready for the next batch. Folks around here love that stuff. It'll sell fast as you can get it in the fruit stand and, honey, yellow squash is like rabbits. It produces faster than you can blink."

"Your granddaughter say she'll play the piano at church startin' this week?" Myrtle asked Hannah.

"I haven't asked her, but I'm sure she will if y'all don't mind her condition or the circumstances. She's pregnant and divorced," Hannah said.

Virgie's giggle was high-pitched. "If she was the first one, we could drown her in the river as an example. If she was the only one, we could shoot her. But she ain't. Besides, seems to me like there's this verse about judging. God knows, I haven't been perfect enough to pass judgment on that."

"I ain't got no problem with it. If my first husband hadn't been willin' to marry me, I would've been in the same fix," Myrtle said.

"Edith?" Hannah asked.

"Honey, if the four of us was to sit down and write up our sins, hers would probably be the least on the list. Why is she divorced?"

"She and this boy had been dating, near as I can get the story straight, about two months, and went out to Vegas on spring break. I don't know the particulars, but they wound up married and woke up the next day wishin' they weren't. So they came home and annulled it, and then she found out she was pregnant. Only he's already engaged to his old high school sweetheart and Kim don't want to tell him."

"Holy moly." Virgie's eyes widened. "That's a mess. Is she really not going to tell him?"

"Says she's not. That it would ruin his marriage and his life." Hannah could hardly believe she was sitting in her kitchen and telling family secrets.

"Smart girl," Edith said. "Well, congratulations. There'll be five generations of you Brewer women."

"If it's a girl," Hannah said.

CHAPTER EIGHT

Karen shut the door on one of the two extra refrigerators in the garage and noticed the edge of an envelope on the top of the fridge. She was surprised to see her name on the outside of the envelope. She tucked it inside the pocket of one of Norma's old stained bibbed aprons, and carried it outside to the front porch to a rocking chair.

"What have you got there?" Kim asked from the rocker on down the row.

An unspoken law had been established from day one about that middle rocker. It had belonged to Norma and now to Hannah and no one ever used it but her.

"It's got my name on it, so I guess it's a letter from Norma. This feels like a scene from *The Twilight Zone*. She buys an expensive piano that she couldn't play, so it had to be for you, and she leaves a letter for me. Here, you read it to me."

Kim ripped into it and held it up to catch the last of the daylight.

Dear Karen,

There are few friendships that transcend the physical and attain unto a higher level. Hannah's and mine had that privilege. I'm glad that you are here and making yourself at home. I'm betting you are ready for a change from the wine business. Women are like that. Give them a task and they conquer it and then move on to the next one. I sincerely hope that you find that challenge here on the farm. I've always thought about making special jams and jellies and having a little shop to sell them. You can't go to the store and buy watermelon rind preserves or fancy spiced peaches. That might not be your new challenge at all, but I'm hoping whatever it is that you grow roots here in Johnston County and love your time here.

Much love,
Norma

Kim handed it back to her. "She's trying to hold us here, isn't she?"

"I believe she is, and the thing that makes it eerie is that it's working. I've wanted to branch out and do something different for years. Now I've got a chance to do so and I'm scared, Kim."

"Don't be scared. The worst thing is that you'll make watermelon rind pickles and they won't sell in the fruit stand, right?"

"Is it time to call my lawyer?" Karen muttered.

"That's better than calling a hit man." Kim giggled. "There's Luke. We've got to feed the donkeys. They are stubborn critters, but I'm making friends with them and by next week, I swear he won't even have to come over here and help me."

"The way you two sparred when we first got here I figured you'd be putting out a hit on him by now," Karen said.

"Ah, he's kind of grown on me. He's not as tacky as he was in the beginning, but I don't reckon anyone will ever get all that cockiness out of him." Kim waved when he got out of the truck.

"About those donkeys: Sell them. The farm doesn't need them. We've got plenty of stubborn without donkeys," Karen said.

Luke heard the last comment as he got out of the truck, and chuckled. "If you read that will Norma left I bet there's a codicil saying that these donkeys can't be killed or harmed in any way. She loved those two old fellers. But you got that right about your granddaughter having her fair share of stubborn."

"Hey, now!" Kim met him halfway and slapped at his arm.

"She's mean too, see?" Luke asked.

Karen waved them away as she went back into the house. "You two children get on out of here and take care of the donkeys."

They walked to the back of the property to the barn and corral. Kim propped one foot on the bottom rung of the fence and talked in a high squeaky voice to Buster, the older donkey with the gray whiskers. "Come on over here and be nice or you won't get this apple."

"Show it to him." Luke broke open a bale of hay in the middle of the corral and Sparky came trotting over from the end of the barn.

She pulled the apple out and Buster ambled toward the fence.

"Now pet him before you give it to him."

She reached out a hand and scratched the donkey's ears. "Soft, aren't they?"

She nodded. "Why did Norma have donkeys? Everything else I can understand. Pigs for bacon and cattle for steaks. And then the garden and orchard, but donkeys?"

Luke put a palm on the top rail and hopped over the fence rather than opening the gate. "They pulled the plow she used to till up her garden. It's the way her dad did things and she just kept on until Grandpa talked her into buying the little tractor. When she found out how much easier it was to work with machinery she bought the bigger one. She promised these two old boys they'd be taken care of until their lives were over when she stopped letting them work. Most of the time she let them roam the back forty with the cattle, but Buster had a cut on his foot and we've been doctoring it before we turn him back out with the steers. Sparky carries on awful if he's not right with Buster, so he had to come along too."

"When will we turn them back out?" she asked.

"Another week and by then they'll be your buddies," Luke answered. "They're over twenty years old; I rode them like horses when I was a kid. I had a real horse at my place, but this was my make-believe pasture, where I was Superman or Batman. And I'll be twenty-five this fall. Grandpa made me go to college in case the little rancher ever got wiped completely out. I teach biology and science at Milburn Junior High."

"Superman? Did you have a cape?" she asked.

"Oh, yeah. Norma made me one out of a worn-out pillow case." He took the apple from her hand and held it out to Buster, who quickly devoured it. Sparky came in an awkward gait from the middle of the pasture and Luke fished a carrot from his pocket for him.

"How long have you been teaching?" Kim asked.

"This will be my second year. What are you going to be when you grow up?"

She smiled up at him. "Well, I was studying business finance so I could go into the hotel business with Nanna. Looks like now I might be a jelly and jam maker and feeder of the donkeys. And, of course, I do keep records up-to-date for the farm, so I guess I'm already grown-up and working."

Luke didn't want to like her. He'd fought it before they arrived and kept fighting it through two whole weeks. This week he'd given up and admitted that he might be wrong. But that did not mean he could kiss her like he wanted to do so badly when he looked down into her eyes. She'd be tired of the new game by fall and she'd be the first one in that van when it headed east. And he'd have nothing but a broken heart. He cleared his throat and looked back at the donkeys.

Kim saw the softness in his eyes and felt the heat between them that had nothing to do with the hot summer wind. And then he blinked and looked away and she wondered if she'd been wrong.

Best if I was, she thought. *Nothing could come of this relationship, not even a good friendship.*

Luke changed the subject. "If you stick around, there's a big festival over in Tishomingo the last weekend in September."

"What kind of festival?"

"The Chickasaw Indian Festival. They gather up over there for a whole week. Something going on every day and then there's a parade on Saturday and free Indian food in the park across Pennington Creek."

Kim did the math in her head. She'd be five months pregnant by then and Luke sure wouldn't want to be seen with her right out in public.

"Guess we'd best be getting on back. Maybe if you're still here we'll take in that festival?"

"I'll be here. Are you asking me out?"

"Would you go with me if I did?" he asked.

"I'd have to think about it."

"Well, you do that, and if the answer is yes, maybe we could have dinner before that festival." He smiled.

He pulled up into the driveway and turned the engine off, ambled around the truck, and opened the door for her. "See you tomorrow evening. Another week and I bet you can go right in the pasture with Buster and Sparky."

"I wouldn't bet on them liking me that soon," she said.

She slung her legs out of the truck and her foot slipped when it hit the ground. One minute she was talking about donkeys, the next the ground was getting closer and closer and then Luke's arms were around her and her cheek was pressed against his chest. His heart was thumping like it had a full head of steam behind it and hers matched his, beat for beat.

He tipped up her chin with his fist and brushed a soft kiss across her lips. The whole sky lit up like the Fourth of July and shivers chased up and down her spine.

Luke took a step back. "Good night, Kim."

"Good night," she mumbled and hurried toward the house.

When she opened the door, Hannah looked up from the kitchen sink, where she was washing tomatoes and setting them on a clean towel.

"You've gotten sunburned running that fruit stand every day. You are using sunblock, aren't you?" she asked.

"Yes, ma'am," Kim said. If her grandmother knew the real reason for her crimson cheeks, she'd be disgusted with her.

Pregnant by one man and kissing another. Not even Nanna would forgive such a thing.

Hannah went on, "Your mother is making marinara sauce in bulk and canning it up in jars. Think it would sell at the fruit stand?"

Sue rustled around in the refrigerator, mainly to cool off her face, but finally pulling out the leftover spaghetti they'd had at supper and putting it in the microwave.

"I think anything sells there. I can't believe how much money that thing pulls in," Kim said.

Sue picked up a huge wooden spoon and stirred a bubbling pot. "Norma had a recipe for it in one of her books. I also found a recipe for salsa and a note that says she sold two gallons of it a day at the stand when she had time to make it. Says it goes for five dollars a pint."

"Did y'all know there's a big Indian festival in Tishomingo at the end of September?" Kim asked.

"It says to squeeze the tomatoes and not add a bit of water." Sue talked as she stirred again. "We need two bay leaves, Italian seasoning, three cloves of garlic, pressed—and the press is in the cabinet above the stove—two onions. The food processor is in the lower cabinet beside the refrigera tor in the garage. Nanna, why would she write down where everything is? Did she have Alzheimer's?"

"I don't think so. Seemed lucid enough to me in her last letters, and the food processor is over there under the tea towel at the back of the cabinet. Edith brought it in for Karen's squash relish," Hannah answered.

Kim watched her mother measure and put the rest of the ingredients into the stockpot and set the burner on simmer.

"Two hours and then pour it into clean, hot jars, cap with flats that have been sitting in boiling water five minutes, twist the rings tight, and cold pack for five minutes," Sue said.

Kim headed toward the piano. Nanna was happy. Her mother was happy and the cellar door was open, so her grandmother was down there again. It sure hadn't taken long to change the Brewer women.

Kim sat down and played "Unchained Melody" Floyd Kramer–style on the piano.

Hannah washed her hands a final time, poured a glass of iced sweet tea, and carried it to the living room. She was tired and it was time to relax. She leaned back and shut her eyes. Before they'd come to Oklahoma, their lives had existed had through phones and touched briefly on holidays. The past weeks had been so wonderful that if she died right then, she would leave without a single regret.

Kim went from one song to the next. Now she was playing the old Patsy Cline classic "Crazy."

Hannah had worked her whole life to provide them with the best, and now she was giving them what was lacking in their lives. That could not be crazy. She'd almost waited too long, but then she and Norma had joined forces and here they were.

Kim played "The Rose," which was another of Hannah's favorites. She opened her eyes and let the lyrics run through her mind. Like the lyrics said, the seed had stayed a long time beneath the coldness, but it was sure hot enough in Oklahoma for it to bloom now.

Sue sat down with a plop on the sofa and pulled a letter from her pocket. "Y'all get one of these?"

"What?" Karen came through the garage with a bowlful of frozen strawberries to thaw for the next day's jelly business.

"A letter. I guess it's from Norma. I found it in the cookbook just now when I was looking for that salsa recipe."

Karen put the bowl beside the sink and sat down beside Sue. "I did. Kind of eerie."

"I read the one for Grandma. Want me to read yours?" Kim asked.

Sue passed it to her. Kim opened it and held it under the piano light. She cleared her throat and started:

Hello Sue,

I'd hoped you would find this. Figured there'd be too many tomatoes to eat and you'd want to make sauce, so I'm leaving it in that page of the cookbook. Hannah has written so much about you. How you like to cook and that you are so independent. I'm glad you are the one who's prowling around in my recipes and keeping the jars filled. John especially likes my spaghetti sauce to be used in the lasagna recipe in this book. Luke is real partial to the rigatoni. And it will sell faster'n hotcakes in the fruit stand if you want to put some down there. You'll find my mother's recipe for Italian bread back toward the back. Makes good garlic bread, and you'll sell every loaf you want to make for the fruit stand.

Love,
Norma

Kim handed the letter back to her mother.

Sue folded it neatly and laid it on the piano. "It's like she was getting ready for all of us, Nanna."

"I think she was," Hannah said. "Check on your sauce and let's go clean out her closet and drawers. It's time and I need the space."

Kim shuddered. "Call Edith. That's a job for you and her friends."

"It's a job for us. You think she wants her dear friends to know if she wore under-britches with stretched elastic or holes in the butt? We'll start with the closet," Hannah said.

"It's weird. You are her soul sister, not us," Kim said.

Hannah stood up. "Weird or not, we're going to do it tonight. What we don't want to keep, we'll put in bags and take to the Goodwill store in Durant."

"How far is it to Durant?" Kim asked.

"It's about twenty miles down the road out there and they've got a Walmart and some shopping. If you want bread and milk, you run into Milburn to the convenience store right across the street from the church and the clinic. If you want to do some real shopping, you go to Durant." Hannah led the way down the hall with three full-grown women shuffling their feet behind her.

Karen sat on the vanity bench.

Sue crawled into the middle of the bed and crossed her legs, Indian-style.

Kim found the farthest corner from the closet and sat on the floor.

Hannah threw open the closet doors and pointed toward several shoe boxes. "We'll start at the top. These are all the letters I've written her since that summer. They are mine and you can't read them until I'm dead and gone. When my things come from the hotel, my letters from her will join these."

"You two kept all those letters? More than sixty years' worth?" Karen asked.

"We did," Hannah said. "And there's a lot of history in them. For one thing, I've put things in those letters I'd never voice out loud, even today. So treat them gently when I'm dead and gone."

"You sure have gotten bossy, Nanna." Kim giggled.

"Yes, I have, and I like the new me. We'll start with clothing. Shirts, which are all fourteens. Denim. Reds. Blues. No pink. That would be because that was Ricky's favorite color on her and she never wore it after that summer. Slacks. Jeans. Six dresses. That should keep me from wearing out the two I brought to use for church and occasions."

Karen put up a palm. "Wait a minute. You can buy anything you want. You're not really going to wear those things, are you?"

Hannah's eyes twinkled. "Of course I am. We shared our things that summer. If you'll look at the picture on the dresser there, that's me in her dress. Why shouldn't I wear these things?"

Kim noticed a picture on the nightstand exactly like the one the lawyer had shown them. "Tell me about this Ricky."

"Who?" Hannah asked.

Kim held up the picture. "The way he and Norma are looking at each other in the picture makes me think something was going on. You know, don't you, Nanna? Norma was in love with that boy. What happened? We want to hear the story."

Hannah sat down on the bed.

"Ricky was about two years old when Norma was born and they were raised up together. They fought like siblings until that summer right before Norma and I both turned seventeen. They'd fallen in love and they were going to get married at the end of the summer. In those days, though, white girls didn't marry Mexican boys. They were sneaking around seeing each other the week I spent here. Then I went home. The rest I know from her letters. Her parents came home early from visiting friends one Sunday afternoon and caught Norma and Ricky…I think you call it making out these days…on the living room sofa. Mr. Andrews sent her to her room with her mother. Ricky vanished. Norma's father was a hard man, like my own father and most all other men of that day. His word was the law and the wife didn't question it. Ricky was gone and she never loved again. After her father died she found out that Ricky had gone to Mexico, married, had a big family, and gotten a very good job."

Kim shook her head. "What a sad story."

"Things were different then. In the forties, it was not going to happen. Her father paraded several respectable men through the house over the years. She refused them all."

Kim sighed. "And they look like they were so much in love. It's terrible the way things work out, isn't it?"

"Yes, it is, and now back to work. There's enough shirts to last me the rest of my days," Hannah said.

"Oh, and you're going to die before the next season's styles come out, are you?" Karen asked.

"Might die tomorrow. I'm keeping these clothes and wearing them. Now dresser drawers. First one, yep, underwear. Size seven. White cotton. Practical."

"Nanna, we cannot give her underpants away. Not even to a mission or a battered women's shelter. It's just not right. Put them over to one side and I'll burn them in the barrel tomorrow morning. I'll go get a garbage sack for things we can't even give away." Kim hurried to the kitchen and brought back a big black trash bag.

Hannah dumped the drawer into the sack. "Never liked cotton, anyway. Second drawer. Nightgowns. In the sack?"

Three heads nodded in agreement.

"Third. Well, take a look at this. Jewelry. Vintage."

Sue leaned over the edge of the bed.

"This must have belonged to her grandmother and her mother. Martha loved jewelry. Even wore it when she was canning beans. I remember these pearl earrings." Hannah held up a pair. "How about it, Sue? In the bag for the burning barrel?"

"Over my dead body. Those things have historical value, and besides, I'm going to wear every piece of that before I die." Sue pulled the drawer from the dresser and dumped the whole thing in the middle of the bed. "I'll untangle every piece if I can have it all."

"Drawers are empty and ready for my things," Hannah said. "Now the chest of drawers. Top one. Socks. I'll keep them. Might get cold this winter. Second one. Tax records for the past hundred years, or so it looks. Guess she used this for a kind of file cabinet. Yep, the rest of the drawers are full of envelopes. Is there room in the file cabinet for this, Kim?"

"No, ma'am. They're full."

"Then we'll buy another one and let them stay right here until we do."

Kim arose like only limber young people can, getting up in one fluid motion. "I'm going take a shower and read until I fall asleep."

Hannah waited until they all left the room, and reached for the first box of letters. She was ready to start reading now that her girls were staying in Oklahoma.

CHAPTER NINE

"Nanna, do you really, really like living like this?" Kim asked as they gathered ripe vegetables in the early morning light.

"I do." Hannah eased up slowly from a bent position, set an old straw hat back on her head, and wiped sweat from her brow. "I feel more alive than I have since…"

"I know…that summer," Kim said.

"Are you having second thoughts about staying out here in this work-infested place? Is the soft life in the green mountains calling to you?" Hannah asked.

"I don't think so. I look back and it was nice. This is just so different."

"Sure is. I haven't heard you talkin' away the hours on your cell phone. Why don't your girlfriends ever call? Used to be you couldn't keep up with all the calls."

"Lacey called once to see if I wanted to go to a concert. I told her I was in Oklahoma on a farm for the summer; that I'd been picking vegetables and cooking, taking care of business on the computer. She didn't believe me. Said she'd run by the hotel and pick me up at three. We'd have an early dinner."

"Did she call back?"

"About three thirty. Madder'n old Buster when I forget his apple in the evening."

"Why?"

Kim carried a bushel of beans to Norma's old work pickup and put them in the back. "Ranted about how she didn't like practical jokes. I tried to tell her I was telling the truth, but she didn't want any part of it. Then a couple of days later Jody e-mailed me that Lacey was still fuming. I sent Jody a note, telling her that I really was in Oklahoma and was thinking about staying here. All I got back was the name of a psychiatrist and his phone number in Morgantown."

"Sounds like they weren't such good friends after all." Hannah put one more tomato on the top of the full bushel basket.

"I'll carry that. Strange thing is I don't have time to miss them. By the time I help you with garden duties and take care of the fruit stand and the bookkeeping duties, there's not much time to play."

"Kim, a woman, no matter how old she is, needs to play some. Shall we have a barbecue or a party on the place? I understand John has one every year over at his ranch. We could rent a band, have some dancing, and call a caterer for food. I bet Edith and Virgie and Myrtle could help plan it."

Kim put the tomatoes in the back of the truck. "That's it for today."

She and Hannah crawled inside, removed their work gloves, and laid them on the seat between them. Kim started up the engine and headed back toward the house at five miles an hour.

"Nanna, I don't need a party. This whole farm thing is more like play than work most days. I love the fruit stand and meeting all the people. It isn't a yearning for Morgantown that scares me. It's the fact that I'm not homesick. It's like I had all that and suddenly this weird thing called Emet, Oklahoma, got a hold of me. Changed me and made me want to live here. We've seen more of each other this past three weeks than we did in my whole life. Momma and I had a fight last night. Even that didn't send me packing. It was like, we had words, but tomorrow we'll cook supper for the guys and everything will be fine because we're together."

She parked in front of the house. Hannah got out of the truck and picked up a bushel of beans. Kim carried a bushel of yellow squash.

Hannah chuckled.

Kim set the squash down and asked, "What's funny?"

"I was laughing at my hands. If Jesse could see them he'd be calling the hotel salon to put in an order for my hair and nails to be done. I had to be perfect all the time, you know," Hannah said.

Kim filled the sink with squash and turned on the water. "But you stayed that way for years after he died."

"Took me a long time to realize that wasn't me," Hannah said.

Kim stuck her hands under the running faucet. "Why'd you bury the real you all those years?"

Hannah looked out the kitchen window. "There's your mom and John, back from moving the irrigation machinery. Whew, I'm glad I'm not him right now."

Kim followed her gaze. "Me too. Her finger gets any closer and she'll be picking his nose. Wonder what put a bumblebee in her britches? Shhh...if you stand right here, you can hear what they are saying."

Hannah smiled. "I've seen her like that, but it's been a very long time. When she throws a fit she can chew up railroad ties and spit out Tinkertoys."

"I didn't even know Momma had a temper," Kim whispered.

Sue had both hands on her hips by then and had raised her voice. "Trying to talk sense to a stubborn man is worse than teaching high school sophomores, and everyone knows they have Teflon-coated brains; everything slides off like fried eggs. I only said there's something haunting about this place. Vintage jewelry, which I love. My mother is whistling when she's making some kind of exotic canned thing. A baby grand piano for Kim. Yet, how did she know we would really come? How'd she know we wouldn't refuse the inheritance or sell this place? She wasn't a witch, was she?"

John folded his arms across his chest. "She wasn't a witch. She was the kindest woman in the world and the smartest."

"But why would an eighty-year-old woman do that? It's as if she's lived through Nanna's life. Like she didn't have one of her own."

"Norma had a full life. She left gifts for you all. Evidently she knew from all those letters she and Hannah exchanged what you all liked, so she tucked them in the right places so you'd find them."

"Like that letter in the cookbook? How do you think I felt seeing my name on a letter like that?"

"Same way Luke and I did when we found one in our mailbox two days after she died. She'd left them with Tillman to be mailed to us. I got cold chills when I got that letter. I don't understand, but she had her reasons."

"Neither do I, and I'm having second thoughts about staying here once the summer is done. That's all I signed on for. To drive Nanna out here and help for the summer. There's something too uncanny about this place. Did she burn black candles and do chants while she read Nanna's letters?"

John's eyes were mere slits and his voice rose louder with each word. "I won't listen to this, Sue. She wasn't that kind of person."

"Of course not. She was an angel with big white wings and a golden halo that floated over her head."

"She was to me," he whispered hoarsely as he turned heel and left her standing on the porch.

"What's the matter with you?" Kim asked when Sue stormed in the back door.

"I'm so mad I could eat cockroaches, and I'm not talking about why, so don't try to wheedle it out of me. I've got salsa to make today, but don't talk to me."

"Yes, ma'am," Kim said.

Sue shook her finger at Kim. "Don't you talk to me in that tone."

"Yes, ma'am," Kim said.

Sue dropped her hand and hugged Kim. "I'm sorry. It isn't your fault."

"I know it isn't. John got under your skin, didn't he?" Kim asked.

"What in the world is going on?" Karen carried two boxes of jars in from the garage.

"Your daughter pitched a fit," Hannah said.

Karen's blue eyes widened. "Sue? She doesn't have a temper, not anymore."

Hannah poured a glass of iced tea. "Guess John aggravated her. Isn't it wonderful?"

Kim leaned against the cabinet. "Twenty minutes until I open the fruit stand. Talk fast so I don't miss anything."

Karen set her boxes on the kitchen table.

Hannah smiled. "She should have done that way back when she was sixteen and something happened that summer you were off in Italy. When you left, she was feisty like most teenagers, showing rebellion and pestering you for a car. When you came back, she acted as if she'd been whipped all the time. When you offered to buy her that little blue car, she set her heels and said she didn't need it. She'd set up a howl for months about a car and then she was refusing it. We should have known then something was wrong."

"I'm right here. Don't talk about me," Sue said.

Hannah held up a palm. "Probably should've taken her to one of those highfalutin therapists. Remember how she rode the bus to school and studied after that? Her grades went from mediocre to excellent. She faced some trauma she didn't share with us. I thought Jeff might rile her up. Marriage does. People can't live together twenty-four hours a day without a good fight every so often, but they did. They made a good couple. Had a good marriage, but there weren't any fireworks in it," Hannah said. "Looks like John opened Pandora's box and let the witch fly right out."

"How old was Momma that summer you are talking about?" Kim looked at Karen.

"She was sixteen that summer right after I got back from Italy." Karen squirmed.

"And we are not discussing that right now. Come on, Mother, we've got a pickup truck to unload and work to do.

And you'd best get on down to the fruit stand, Kim. I do believe I hear the ladies coming. Nanna, we need to pay them for all their help," Sue said.

"I tried, but they won't have it. Said they used to come over and help Norma and they're just glad to have a place to come to gossip like they did when she was alive."

❖ ❖ ❖

Tension hung over the whole patio like smoke in a cheap corner bar.

Kim looked from her mother to John.

Luke poked her on the arm. "Are our children fighting?"

She winked.

Supper was served buffet style. Sue had covered a folding table with a red-and-white checkered plastic tablecloth and arranged a bowl of fresh garden salad, lasagna, hot garlic bread, and all the dinnerware around a quart jar filled with flowers she'd gathered from the flower bed that afternoon. She and Karen had carved a watermelon to look like a whale, hollowed out the inside, and refilled it with watermelon and cantaloupe balls, strawberries and peaches.

Everyone was eating as if it was their last meal except Sue and John, who picked at their food and acted like sulking teenagers.

"So what's been happening over here this week?" Luke asked.

Karen held up her hand like a schoolchild. "I called my lawyer last week and told him to proceed with the divorce just like my husband wants. Only thing is if he wants my half of the business, he has to buy my house too. And I set the price very, very high. If he wants it so bad, he can find a financer. Figure if he buys, that's the sign I should definitely go on with my plans to stay."

Hannah touched Karen on the shoulder. "What did you just say?"

"You can leave me the farm if the other two don't want their shares. I'm staying. Mother, does that make you happy?"

"Yes, it does, and I am proud of you, but the important question is did it make you happy?" Hannah asked.

"Oh, yes, very happy."

"Then it's good. Who's next?" Hannah asked.

Kim was shocked. Part of being a perfect Brewer was never, ever hanging the family laundry on the clothesline. Her grandmother had just made an announcement that would have been told behind closed doors in West Virginia. Guards would stand in front of the doors and the four women around the conference table would prick their fingers and sign a document in blood that said they'd never tell what they'd heard.

Karen held up her hand again. "I'm not finished. Now that I'm out from the middle of the forest, I can see the trees. They aren't very pretty. I don't want to dwell on them or look at them anymore. There's a lot of living in this old girl. You told me so, Mother, and you don't lie. I'm going to start a little store that stays open in the winter to sell my stuff in, maybe in the front part of the garage."

John didn't hold up his hand for permission to speak. "Thank you for a lovely supper. I think I'll forgo games tonight. I'm tired."

"I don't think so," Sue said tensely. "We're playing poker and I will own your cattle operation by the time the night is over."

"Pretty sure of yourself, aren't you?" John said coolly.

"I know when I'm right." She glared across the table at him.

His green eyes narrowed into slits. "Luke, go get the cards. This woman needs to be taught a lesson. Before the night is done I'll own her share of this farm."

Kim held up her hand like a dutiful second grader. "Sounds to me like a grudge match. Why don't you two take a walk and clear the air? No guns, knives, or blunt objects allowed. Don't come back until the fight is settled."

Sue pointed at her daughter. "I'm not a teenager. Don't you dare talk to me like that."

Kim raised both eyebrows. "Well, you are both acting like you are. You have been sulking all day. I don't care if you take guns, knives, or blunt objects. Get out of here and don't come back until you get it out of your system. May the best man or woman win, and whoever is alive has to bury the other one."

"You don't tell me what to do. I'm the mother," Sue said.

Hannah snapped her fingers. "Enough. Susanna, you and John kiss and make up or get out of here until you can work out your problems. I'm retiring into the living room and watching *Law and Order* on television. Mosquitoes are getting around the citronella candles and biting me. Luke, you and Kim can do the cleanup. Karen, you are watching television with me."

Sue blushed from the top of her forehead to the tips of her toes. She stood up and started down the lane toward the fruit stand. Without a word, John followed her.

Kim and Luke gathered up dishes and headed toward the kitchen.

"Think they'll work it out?" Luke asked.

"I hope so. I've never seen my mother act like this," Kim answered.

"Well, I've never seen John like this either. He's dated women lots of times and even was engaged once."

Kim shot a squirt of soap into the dishwater as it ran. "Tell me about it."

"Not much to tell. They dated about six months and he asked her to marry him and she said yes. Then he found out that she'd been cheatin' on him and it was over. Can't blame him."

Kim handed him the dish towel and their fingertips brushed, creating the same old tingle as before. Fate was a witch!

Sue and John walked beside each other, their bodies not a foot apart. When they reached the fruit stand she opened the small door at the end and stood to one side. He didn't budge, so she went into the tiny building, plopped down in a chair, and folded her arms across her chest.

He pulled up the flap over the front window and secured it with the latches, sat down beside her, propped his boots up on the shelf that normally held the vegetables for sale, and looked straight ahead. The sun set in a blaze of orange, yellow, and pink. Beautiful sunsets were one of the many things Oklahoma had bragging rights to. Sue had never seen such a splash of color as nature presented every evening.

"Still mad?" John asked.

"I could take on a forest fire with a cup of water."

"Then we'll wait some more."

Darkness fell and a full moon hung in the sky right above tree level. Stars began to pop out like diamonds pushing their way through an indigo velvet cape. A few clouds scooted around, but not one had the nerve to cover the moon. John stood up and, for a minute, Sue thought he'd gotten bored and was leaving. She didn't care if he did. She didn't know what she wanted, wouldn't recognize it if she got it, so he couldn't produce it—whatever *it* was. If John walked barefoot on a barbed-wire fence, sang her favorite song, and offered her a dozen red roses, she still wouldn't be happy.

He waited thirty minutes before he said a word, and then it was only two: "Any better?"

"Little bit."

"We'll wait awhile longer."

In a few minutes, John reached over to Kim's CD player and poked the radio button.

He stood and offered her his hand. "May I have this dance?"

"I might bite you," she said but she put her hand is his.

"I'll take my chances," he said.

When he drew her close, her ear was right on his heart and she could hear a good, strong, steady heartbeat. Darryl Worley was singing, "I Miss My Friend," as he two-stepped with her inside the confines of the tiny fruit stand. The lyrics said he missed the color that she brought into his life and the silly fights and the late-afternoon walks.

Sue missed that too. She missed her new friend and the relationship they'd built since day one. She had lived in indifference covered with thinly veiled happiness for entirely too long and she didn't like it. But she didn't like the anger she'd lived with all day either. There had to be a happy medium in there somewhere.

"How's it going?" he whispered.

"I'm not going to explode. It was touch and go for a while," she said.

"We'll dance a while longer."

The next song on the radio was by Blake Shelton: "She Doesn't Know She's Got It." John grabbed one hand and swung her around until she giggled. His boots were like lightning on the wooden fruit stand floor.

"It's true, you know. You've got it and you don't even know it," he said.

"I'm almost forty, John."

"So? I'm almost forty-five. You think we can't still have it?"

"You are crazy."

The song ended and the next one was a slow waltz by George Jones: "I Always Get Lucky With You." John swung her around to his chest and barely moved around the floor.

A commercial for a car company in Ardmore, Oklahoma, came on next, so he bowed and thanked her for the dances, bringing her fingertips to his lips for a kiss.

"Better now?" he asked.

"Yes, thank you."

"Want to talk about it?"

"I'm not ready to be a grandmother. I'm mad because I never got to be angry at some bad things in my life. A terrible thing happened the year I was sixteen, and another, a couple of years ago. My heart was numb, but it never got angry, and now it is."

"I'd give half my ranch to have a daughter like Kim and grandchildren," he said wistfully.

"Really? Why didn't you ever marry?"

"Didn't find the right woman," he said.

She sighed. "Norma got the blame today. It's just weird the way things are here. All four of us have found our peace and it scares the bejesus out of me. Did you hear what my mother said? She's going to stay and she's already called the lawyers. By the end of the summer, the divorce will be over. She's starting a new venture and she's all excited. Time is passing me by. I've been so busy protecting my heart that I forgot to live."

"Then make up for lost time," he said.

"How? I'm going to be a grandmother and I'm not ready to be that old."

"Be a young one. There's not a place in the Good Book that says, 'Thou hast to be old to be a grandmother.' It's a matter of setting your mind. You can wither up and die or be young until you die. Miss Norma's body aged and quit working, but she never got old."

"Like Nanna?"

"They're two of a kind."

"Did you know she had a bad heart?"

"No, not until I got my letter. She explained that the day she bought the piano she'd been to the heart doctor. He said she needed open-heart surgery and she needed to give up her cigarettes. He said she wouldn't live six months without the heart operation and not more than three if she kept smoking."

"She was a smoker? I thought she was perfect. We didn't smell smoke in the house."

"That's because she smoked on the patio. And she was far from perfect. Opinionated. Hardheaded. Mean as a snake if someone crossed her. Soft as a lamb if she loved you. I don't think either of those women wanted to really see the other one. If they did, they'd have to admit they weren't seventeen anymore. It was their way of staying forever young. She knew you'd come because she wanted you to, and she got what she wanted. It was God's way of making it up to her because she couldn't marry Ricky."

"You know about him?"

"Sure. She told me all about him one evening about six months ago."

"Why did we fight?" she asked.

"Because you needed to, and it's been a long time since I got my blood pressure up like that. Does a man good sometimes. Cleans out the arteries."

"Think we'll argue again?" She looked at the moon through the glass.

"Oh, yeah, we are two passionate people, and that brings out fights."

"I'm not sure I like it."

"Just remember that passion also brings out something other than arguments. Ready to go home now?"

"*Home?* Sounds strange. Home has been Morgantown since I was born. How could all that change in just a few weeks?"

"Because Miss Norma wanted it and God has a special place in his heart for those who've been denied love." He offered his hand.

She took it and it felt right when he laced his fingers with hers.

"I could have owned your cattle ranch," she said when he walked her to the front door.

"I would have owned your share of this operation," he declared.

"I'm really good at poker."

"I'm better."

"Someday we'll play and you'll lose your shirt."

He brought her hand to his lips and kissed her fingertips again. "I'm looking forward to it."

She shivered in spite of the Oklahoma heat and waited for the goose bumps to fade before she went inside.

"So do you need someone to help you bury the body?" Kim asked.

"I didn't kill him," Sue answered. "I think I'm over my hissy fit, though. Sorry if I ruined the evening."

"Don't apologize. It could be the first time you ever did anything that wasn't perfect," Kim said.

Sue laughed. "Kim, if the baby is a girl, would you think about naming her Norma?"

"I like old names. They have character. Sounds good to me. Maybe we'll call her Norie for short. And if it's a boy?"

"Brewer women haven't been too good in that department up to now." Sue crossed the room and gave Kim a hug.

CHAPTER TEN

"Well, Norma, let's go to town," Hannah talked to the empty seat next to her. "I think I've got everything figured out, but I wanted to talk to you about it, and I don't want those three to eavesdrop or to think I've really lost my mind."

She clutched and shifted into reverse, then let up on the clutch and pushed down on the gas pedal. The truck did little bunny hops, but it didn't stall. She let up on the gas, stomped the clutch, and shifted into first. This time it moved forward smoothly. Driving carefully all the way to the end of the lane in first, she braked, forgot to clutch, and the truck died.

"Dang it. You could help me, Norma," Hannah fussed as she turned the key.

When she reached Milburn she had gotten the feel of the truck. The clutch was a little loose, but she didn't have to remind herself to use it every time she shifted gears. Like riding a bicycle, it all came back to her as she drove. The music was just right, and she bobbled her head in time to the loud noise.

"I'm glad you left me some of your old friends, but why didn't you put some friends in the path for the girls? Kim, especially, at her age?"

She waited and nodded.

"I see. Kim needs to lean on Luke and if she had a bunch of girlfriends then she wouldn't have time to form a relationship with him. And the same with Sue. But what about Karen?"

She waited, but nothing came.

"Guess we'll discuss that one later."

The town of Milburn was contained on two sides of one block. Church on one corner. Big two-story house right across the street. Gas station, convenience store, and burger shop all rolled into one diagonally across the street from the church. Medical clinic across from the store with the community center next to the clinic. Hannah parked in the lot at the convenience store and went inside.

She'd set two gallons of milk on the cashier's counter and opened her purse to get out her wallet when the man behind her tapped her on the shoulder.

"Well, hello, Hannah."

She didn't recognize him.

"Tillman, the lawyer who made up your will. You did get your copy in the mail, didn't you?"

She nodded. "I'm sorry. You look different out of that suit."

"I'm on my way to the lake for a day on my boat," he said. "And how is your daughter?"

"Karen?"

"Yes, the pretty one," he said.

"She's fine," Hannah answered.

"Well, tell her hello for me." And he disappeared around the end of the aisle.

"Well, ask for a fish and get a whale." Hannah giggled.

She toted her milk out to the truck and put it in the passenger's seat. She looked over at the milk and smiled. "You can hold that for me. Don't you dare spill it. I bet you are giggling right now. Did you plan that one too or is it an added bonus?"

The truck sputtered once when she backed it out of the parking lot, but she was talking to Norma and didn't even fuss about it. When she got home, her friends were there and Karen, Sue, and Kim met her at the truck.

Karen's expression looked like she'd been sucking on lemons. "Where have you been?"

"I got milk. You can unload it. Oh, and I brought home a compliment for you. That lawyer that came out here said that you were the pretty one."

"Well, he's full of crap and you shouldn't be driving and you dang sure shouldn't be going off alone in that old rattle-trap truck and..." Karen stopped for a breath.

Hannah started before she could, "I'm eighty years old. I can go and come as I please without telling any of you and if I want to drive that old rattletrap to Dallas and go shopping all by myself I'll dang sure do it."

"Well, when you do I hope you find a beauty shop," Sue said.

"I'm not cutting my hair. I like Edith's, thrown up in a ponytail, pulled back through the hole in a ball cap. Looks real cute and will keep it off my neck. I figure by the end of summer, it'll be long enough to do that."

"I didn't even know you could drive," Kim said.

"Last time was when Sue was born. I drove the Caddy to the hospital to see you and the baby the day after she was born. I tail-ended that Ford at a stoplight. The crazy woman stopped so quick it's a wonder she didn't drop her transmission on the pavement, and I crawled right up in her trunk. Jesse never bought another car after that. Anyplace I wanted to go, he had one of the hired help at the hotel drive me. I've served a near forty-year sentence, and today I got out of prison."

"Good for you, Nanna," Kim said.

"Now unload that milk and bring it in. My friends are probably already sorting vegetables and I've got to tell them my story about driving again." Hannah marched off toward the house.

❖ ❖ ❖

Kim propped her bare feet up on the porch railing. She'd taken a shower and changed into cutoff overalls and a tank top. Luke would be there anytime, and tonight they were turning Buster and Sparky back into the pasture with the cattle. Luke had spotted a coyote on his property, and the donkeys would protect the calves from coyotes.

She heard a vehicle and was about to stand up when it pulled up into the yard. It wasn't Luke's truck, and she didn't recognize the car. Maybe Edith or Virgie had gotten a new vehicle and come to show it off to Hannah. She shaded her face with her hand and could scarcely believe her eyes.

"Holy crap! What is Grandpa doing in Emet, Oklahoma?"

"Kim?" His eyes went from her bare feet to the braids hanging down to her shoulders.

"Grandpa? What are you doing here?"

His nose curled. "I came to talk to your grandmother."

"Hey, Grandma!" Kim yelled at the top of her lungs.

Karen poked her head out the front door and Daniel's nose did a full snarl. Karen wore denim shorts, a knit shirt, and flip-flops. Her hair was pulled back in a ponytail and she didn't have a drop of makeup on. She'd been working in cucumbers all day, making various kinds of pickles, so Eau de Vinegar wafted out from her.

Daniel sneezed. "My God, woman, what happened to you?"

"You did," she said.

"Can we talk privately?"

Karen stepped out on the porch. "No, but we can talk in front of Kim. I'd offer you something to drink, but you won't be here that long."

"Hello, Daddy." Sue came around the end of the house. "What brings you out slumming?"

Hannah followed her. "Daniel?"

Daniel leaned against the car. "You have all gone crazy. This isn't you, Karen. How do you live in this heat? And why do you live in this hovel?"

He ran a finger around the inside of his white shirt collar, pulled a monogrammed handkerchief from the pocket of his jacket, and wiped his hand.

"Karen, I've got to talk to you, and I'd rather it be private… please?"

She sat down in one of the rocking chairs. "I've found my mind, and you get used to the heat. The house is smaller than the one I've got up for sale in Virginia, but it's home. And say what you've got to say. I'm listening."

"I want to just talk to you, not the whole family."

"Too bad. Whatever you've got to say will be said in front of all of us, or else you can get in your rental and drive back to the airport. Your choice," Karen said.

"Tiffany know you are here with your wife?" Kim asked.

"Yes, she does. She realizes we are going to have to get this business over. She trusts me. I wouldn't betray that," he said.

"Well, ain't that nice. You've finally changed in your old age," Karen said.

Daniel ran his fingers through his hair. "I don't want to fight. I want the winery. I want the label and all of it. Tiffany does not want the house. She had her heart set on something new that doesn't have your ghost in it. You can't be serious about staying in this hole in the road. You will wither up and die in this dusty place."

"The agreement is that you take it all within thirty days or I put it on the market and you can have a new partner. There are a few Italians I can call who would be interested in the house and my half of the winery and who'll meet my price," she said.

Daniel smiled and his voice softened. "Come on, Karen, be reasonable. Keep the house. You aren't really going to stay out here in this godforsaken place, are you?"

Karen went on, "I'm not selling my half without the buyer taking the house. Maybe you'd sell your half at the same time I do to one of my Italian friends? That way you and Tiffany could just play until the money is gone. Bet you diamonds to cow piles she can go through it all in ten years. That would make you a pauper in your old age, wouldn't it?"

He leaned against the car, but the metal was so hot, he didn't stay long. "Karen, you have always been reasonable. What has happened to you?"

"Oklahoma happened to me. I love it here," she answered.

He wiped at his forehead every ten seconds with the damp handkerchief. "You can't be serious. This really is a hovel compared to what you're used to. Admit it. You miss your friends and your home and the staff to take care of the house." He took in the house, flower beds, shade tree, and all with a wave of his hands.

"Darlin', this is paradise compared to what I was used to. I don't have to wonder if the woman I'm having lunch with has been to bed with you," she told him. "I've got a brand-new challenge, and honey, I love all of my new life."

"Tiff wants to build one of those new glass-and-chrome things." Daniel put on his sweet voice. "Be reasonable. Sell me your half of the winery and move back home, into your house."

Karen shook her head. "Well, this time she'll have to make do with a big old plantation house. I'm sure all your children will grow up just fine there. Sue did. Is that all you came to discuss?"

"You won't budge?" Daniel tried once more.

"I won't budge an inch, darlin'."

"What are you going to do with that much money? Build a house in this place and be a big fish in a mud puddle?" His sweet voice had been replaced by a low growl.

Karen gave him her brightest smile. "Not this year. Maybe later when the donkeys die I'll pick out a spot and build something back in their part of the property, but as long as we all don't start pulling each other's hair out, then I expect we'll live right here together. Oh, and I've got some news. I'm going to be a great-grandmother."

"And you'll be a great-grandfather," Kim said.

He ran his fingers through his damp hair. "You are kidding me. Are you having the baby? There are places you could go."

Kim shook her head. "That's not the way Momma raised me."

"I can't believe you've turned into hicks in so short a time. My lawyer will be in touch," he growled.

"Have a safe trip back, Grandpa," Kim said sweetly.

"Let me know when you want to take possession of the house. I'll have the movers come pack up and bring everything out here," she said.

He stopped dead in his tracks, the door open in his hands. "You're going to take everything out of it?"

"Of course, you didn't think you were getting all my grandparents' heirlooms for that price, did you?"

"Everything?" he asked.

"All of it."

"I want to take possession in thirty days, then," he said.

"It'll be cleaned out by then, and it's a wise decision. I'm sure Tiffany will want to refurnish it in her glass and brass, or is it pewter and glass? I'll leave the kitchen appliances, the washer and dryer, and the freezers. Other than that, there won't be a hairpin left in the house. You might want to have a meeting with the staff too. Tiffany will want her own gardeners and domestic help."

"Why are you doing this?" His voice had changed to a deep whine.

"I'm just settling my affairs out there so I can start a new life here, Daniel. Tiffany can choose her own furniture. She sure wouldn't like an eighteenth-century oak sideboard, now, would she?"

He shivered in spite of the heat. "God, this is a nightmare."

"Darlin', you should have thought about that when you were cheatin'. It's time to reap what you sowed," Karen said.

"I hope you are miserable in this hellhole." He slammed the door before she could answer and peeled out of the driveway, throwing gravel all over the place.

Sue reached over and took Karen's hand in hers. They sat there until the dust settled from Daniel's departure. Locusts sang. A blue jay fussed at a squirrel. Hot wind brushed across their faces. A few clouds drifted slowly across a summer blue sky. Peace returned.

"Well, that went well, didn't it?" Sue finally whispered.

"I don't think it could have been better," Hannah said.

"You OK, Grandma?" Kim looked at Karen.

Karen smiled brightly. "Never been better. Where do you figure we'll have to go to find a great big storage unit?"

"You're really doing this?" Hannah asked.

"I am," Karen said. "Daniel thought he could sweet-talk me into doing just what he wanted. I didn't cave in, and for the first time in years, I feel like I'm in control of my life."

Hannah patted her shoulder. "There's storage units in Tishomingo and Durant both. Like you said, a lot of your furniture is antique, so you'd best get one of those climate-controlled things. You'll have to rent more than one, but what will you do with all that stuff?"

"Eventually, I will build my own house on down the lane toward the back of the property and maybe even have a small factory with a store out in front. Someday when it feels like the right time. I'm not in a hurry, and my things will be fine in storage. Now let's go in the house where it's cool. I'm sweating like a long-tailed cat in a room full of rocking chairs."

Hannah threw back her head and laughed. Lord, it was good to be alive and happy.

CHAPTER ELEVEN

Kim watched the screen as the ultrasound technician ran a magic wand over her still-flat belly. The woman adjusted the volume and a swooshing sound filled the room at the same time a little heart appeared on the screen along with a loud thumping noise.

"The noise is the heartbeat and…" The technician cocked her head to one side and then the other. "And that's another heartbeat, and that is your other baby."

Kim's eyes were glued to the tiny valentine heart on the screen and the words went right over her head. She was really going to be a mother, and there was the little heart to prove it.

"Did you hear me? I said you are having twins, either boys or girls because they are sharing a sac," the lady said.

Kim raised her eyes from the screen and gasped. "But there's only one heart."

The lady smiled. "There are two heartbeats. I hear them both very clearly, and they're strong."

Her eyes went back to the monitor. How could there be two babies in there when she couldn't even see one?

"I'm printing a copy of the ultrasound for you to take home. See where the cursor arrow is? That's your twins. One right here and one curled up right in front of him or her. Looks like they are already friends."

Kim squeezed tears back, refusing to let them stream down her cheeks.

The woman wiped the jelly from her belly and laid the picture on the table. "You can get dressed now. I'll send these results to your doctor, and I'm sure after your next visit, she'll want to see you more often than once a month since you are having twins."

"Thank you," Kim mumbled.

She picked up the picture and unfocused her eyes. It looked like a funnel with the top chopped off. Maybe she was holding it upside down. She flipped it and still it only looked like shades of gray swirls.

When she was dressed, she picked up her purse and picture and carried them to the waiting room, where Hannah, Karen, and Sue all waited. Her mother looked up and raised an eyebrow.

Kim slumped into a chair, handed Sue the picture, buried her face in Hannah's shoulder, and wept.

Hannah put both arms around her and patted her on the back. "Kim, what is it? Is the baby all right? What happened in there?"

Kim finally got control of the sobs, took the picture from Sue's hand, and handed it to Hannah. She wiped at tears with her shirtsleeve, but they still flowed freely. "Look at that, Nanna. It's a picture of my babies and I can't even see them. I'm going to be a terrible mother. I can't even find them in that funnel."

"Well, I can't see anything but a fuzzy blurb," Hannah said.

Kim gave her cheek another swipe. "I know!"

Karen patted her on the leg. "Darlin', I can't ever find a blessed thing in one of those either. I'm sure there is a baby in all those lines but you've got to remember, it's not much bigger than a peanut right now."

Sue slung an arm around her. "That doesn't mean you're going to be a bad mother. When the baby is big enough to fill up that funnel, then you'll be able to see it."

"But you'd think if there was two of them that I could at least see one." Kim sniffled.

"Twins?" Hannah whispered.

Kim nodded and frowned at the picture. "And I still can't find either one of them."

Karen giggled nervously. "Me either. Did they hear two heartbeats?"

Kim turned the picture upside down. "She said she did and that they were in the same sac, so it's either two boys or two girls."

Sue snatched the picture from Hannah. "Right there. See. They are facing each other."

Kim focused until her head threatened to split. "Where?"

Sue pointed to the break in the swirling pattern.

"*That* is babies?" Kim asked.

"Yes, it is."

She finally smiled. "We need a frame. It's their first picture."

"Right after lunch we'll go buy a frame, but first we eat," Hannah said. "Chili's?"

"Sounds wonderful," Kim agreed.

"You are a lucky woman," Karen told her on the way outside. "When I was pregnant with your mother, I had morning sickness the whole nine months, and you are eating anything you want."

Sue raised her hand as soon as she fastened her seat belt. "Me too. Only I was only sick three months. After that first trimester, it went away and I craved pizza for six months."

"Nanna?" Kim asked.

"Sick as a dog with Karen for about four months and then it was over," Hannah said and then changed the subject. "What have you been craving?"

Kim shrugged. "Nothing yet. Maybe later. I'll be glad when they're bigger and I can see real babies. Oh my God! It's twins."

Karen laughed. "Just now hit you, didn't it?"

Kim swallowed hard. "I don't even know how to take care of one baby. How am I going to take care of two? Momma, you have to stay and help me. I'll do something horribly wrong if you aren't here."

Sue started the engine and backed out of the parking lot. "You will do fine. Two is just twice the work, but there's no way I'll leave now if you are staying here. I'll call my principal and tell him I'm sending my resignation. How should I take care of the house? I'll need to go back and pack everything and put it on the market, but the peaches are ready to harvest, then it'll be the apples. No wonder Norma never had time to leave town."

Karen piped up from the backseat. "Do what I did. Call the movers and have them go in and pack everything. There are still empty storage areas where I've got my stuff stored."

Sue found a parking space close to the door at Chili's and looked in the rearview at Hannah. "Nanna, if we're going to live here permanently, I'd like some of my own things around me. We could put the sofa in the living room down in the wine cellar and use my living room outfit."

"Norma wouldn't care if you gutted the place and replaced everything. She wanted us to live here but that kind of thing didn't matter," Hannah said.

Kim raised an eyebrow. "Oh, and after not seeing her for more than sixty years, you know exactly what she'd think or what would matter?"

Hannah hit the button to open the door. "No, that ESP stuff was Norma's field. Mostly I'm in the dark, but I'm figuring out a lot of things as I go along. Hindsight is twenty-twenty, as they say," Hannah said.

The lunch rush hadn't started, so the waitress seated them immediately and before Sue even settled into the booth beside Kim her phone rang. She fished it out of her purse and whispered, "Hello."

"You can talk out loud, Momma." Kim laughed.

Sue blushed. "We're in a restaurant. That's horrible manners."

"Yes, it is, so I won't talk but a minute," John chuckled. "Would you like to go with me to dinner this evening? Fish Tales serves up a fine buffet of seafood over in Tishomingo."

"Yes, I would," Sue said. "What time? We are in Durant, but we'll be home in a couple of hours."

"Pick you up at seven. See you later."

Kim poked her mother on the arm. "You've got a date. I'm jealous. I'd love to be going out with Luke."

"Why don't you?" Karen asked. "He's definitely interested."

She pointed at her stomach. "Twins."

"What's the difference to him if it's one or two?" Hannah asked.

"She hasn't even told him about one yet, have you?" Sue asked.

Hannah gave her a serious look from across the table. "I'd say you'd better tell him pretty quick, girl. John knows. Edith and the ladies all know, and believe me, as small as Emet is, I'm surprised that someone hasn't already told him."

"But what if…" Kim sputtered.

"You'll never know if you don't talk to him," Hannah said. "Now let's order and do some shopping. We need a picture frame from Walmart, and there's some really nice shops down on Main Street."

❖ ❖ ❖

Kim was sitting on the porch when John arrived. She waved from the rocking chair at the end of the row and he propped a hip on the rail. His jeans had been ironed to a shiny finish and creased perfectly. His boots shined and his shirt was tucked in behind a silver-laced black belt with a big silver buckle.

"Doctor visit go all right?" he asked.

"It's twins," she said.

He chuckled. "Double trouble."

"Momma said she'll stay in Emet to help me. She's sending in her resignation to the school."

His face lit up. "Good news all around, I'd say."

Sue opened the door and stepped outside. She wore a new blue sundress and cute little sandals. Her perfume wafted out in the hot evening breeze as she crossed the porch. "I thought I heard a man's voice out here."

"You look beautiful," John said.

Her blush rivaled the red sky around the brilliant sunset. "You look pretty fine yourself."

"You two better be home before the clock strikes midnight or you'll be grouchy tomorrow," Kim teased.

"I'm not Cinderella," Sue said.

"Well, you look like a modern-day princess to me," Kim said.

"Does she turn into a pumpkin at midnight?" John asked.

"No, but if you don't have her home by curfew, your pickup will and the tires will be gophers," Kim said.

"I thought they were mice," Sue argued.

"Not on a truck with Oklahoma tags. They are gophers, so you'd better get home by midnight."

Luke's truck came to a stop beside John's and he crawled out of the driver's seat. His blond hair looked like it had been combed with a hay rake, his shirt was dusty, and his jeans had a hole in the knee.

"Hey, where are y'all goin' all duded up?" he asked.

"Out to dinner at Fish Tales."

"Well, thanks so much for inviting me and Kim to go with you," he said.

Kim motioned for him to join her in the rocking chair lineup. "Sometimes the children earn the right to go out by themselves."

"Did you tell them when they have to be home?" Luke teased.

"I did. Truck turns into a pumpkin at midnight," Kim answered.

Luke brushed back a lock of hair from his sweaty forehead. "Well, you heard the lady. Midnight it is."

John chuckled. "Don't wait up. I know the way home if the gophers take off and my truck turns into a pumpkin."

"Hungry?" Kim asked when the truck was out of sight.

"Just had a gourmet meal over at my place," he said.

"And you didn't invite me?"

Luke shook his head. "Nope."

"Some friend you are. What was it?"

Luke gave her a wickedly sexy grin. "Well, it takes a long time to prepare. You want details?"

"I do."

The grin got bigger. "I like the sound of that."

Kim shrugged. "I've always liked cooking. Momma and I spent a lot of time together in the kitchen, so start from the beginning."

Luke chuckled.

"What?"

"Your hair is brown, but sometimes I think you have blonde roots," he said.

She reached up and touched her hair. "I've never dyed my hair. Oh! I get it! You were grinning because I said 'I do.'"

"Yes, I was but back to my gourmet meal. First, you put mayonnaise on three slices of bread. One side only, and then you put pepper jack cheese on two pieces of the bread and bologna on the third one. Now, this is where it gets tricky. You put sliced tomatoes, lettuce leaves, and dill pickles on one cheese piece and top that with another slice of bologna, then slap on the bread with the bologna on it, add another layer of tomatoes, lettuce, and dill pickles, and the last piece with cheese on it. Know why you do it that way?"

"Of course, so the tomato doesn't make the bread soggy. My dad was an expert at making Dagwood sandwiches," she said.

"Well, rats! I thought the invention belonged to me. How did the Durant trip go today?"

Kim swallowed hard. "How did you know we went to Durant?"

"Fruit stand was closed and I'm out of strawberry jam."

"Do you eat that on everything?" she asked.

The killer smile was back. "Except my gourmet sandwiches and tacos. It's wonderful on ice cream and waffles. So?" He raised an eyebrow.

She swallowed hard again. "What? Oh, the Durant trip?"

He nodded.

"I'm pregnant and it's twins."

"I know. And everything is fine?" Luke asked.

Kim jerked her head around so quickly that she set the rocking chair in motion. "You know! You know!" she repeated.

"I know. I know!"

"How long have you known?"

He chuckled again. "A while, and you'll never guess what the big news is in Emet. Want to try?"

She was too flabbergasted to speak so she shook her head.

"That the baby is mine. I mean babies."

"But..." she stammered.

"Cute, ain't it?"

"But you know that's not true."

"I do," he said and then burst out laughing.

CHAPTER TWELVE

Kim threw a pillow on the floor, stretched out on the hardwood floor, and sighed.

Hannah looked down on her from the end of the sofa and asked, "Who poured sour milk on your oatmeal this morning?"

Sue poked her head in from the kitchen. "She's been in a mood all day, hasn't she? Must be hormones kicking in."

Karen sunk down on the other end of the sofa and propped her feet on the coffee table. "It doesn't have a thing to do with hormones. She's mad at you, Sue."

"What'd I do?" Sue asked.

"You went out on a real date with John and when you all left she came in here all puffed up like a bullfrog and has been in a Jesus mood ever since."

"What's a Jesus mood?" Kim asked.

"It's when Jesus Himself couldn't live with you," Hannah answered.

Kim raised up on one elbow. "You are all wrong. I'm not hormonal. I'm not mad at Momma. I think it's great she and John are getting along and dating, and personally, I think Daddy would be fine with it. I'm mad enough to eat cockroaches—your expression, Momma, and it fits well because Luke laughed at me."

"Want to tell us about it?" Hannah asked.

"Or sulk another day or two?" Sue piped up right behind her.

"I told him I was pregnant with twins and he thought it was funny. I got mad and stormed into the house and he left and I can be mad for a week if I want to," Kim said.

Luke poked his head in the back door and yelled. "Should I throw my hat in first or is it safe in there?"

"It's not safe and I'll be right out." Kim yelled back.

"And?" Hannah asked.

"Keep the shovels ready." Kim smiled.

She went straight to the rocking chairs and sat down.

Luke followed her and sat in the one on the other end, leaving Hannah's empty. He'd come straight from hay hauling and had straw still stuck in his hair. His boots were scuffed, his jeans were dusty, and the bandanna hanging out of his pocket was limp from wiping sweat all day.

"You still carryin' a grudge because I laughed?"

"I carry a grudge for a while."

"Longer than it takes me to go home and get cleaned up?"

"Probably."

"Have I told you lately that you are beautiful, Miss Kim DeHaven?"

"Are you flirting?" Kim turned to find him staring right at her.

Luke didn't blink. "Could be. Is it working?"

"I told you I am pregnant. We got married in Vegas and had it annulled two days later. He doesn't even know about the babies," she said.

"I told you that I already knew that. His loss. My gain," Luke said. "Want to go with me to the Fourth of July fireworks tomorrow night?"

"Did you not hear a word I said?"

He moved to the porch railing right in front of her and leaned forward. He tipped her head up with his fist and looked right into her eyes. "I heard every single word of it and I'm glad that you are pregnant. I thought you were running from me because I'm just a teacher and a rancher. Now, you want to run into Milburn for a snow cone?"

"I'd kill for a snow cone," she whispered.

He brushed a soft kiss across her lips and laced his fingers in hers. "Hot night. Pretty woman. Let's drive all the way to Durant for that snow cone."

"I'm going to get fat, very fat," Kim said.

He pulled her up and led her to his truck. "Not on one snow cone."

"Are you for real?"

He grinned. "Yes, ma'am, I am. You need some help at the fruit stand? I could come over in the afternoons and relieve you an hour or two."

"I can work all summer. They aren't due until February," she said.

He was supposed to be running all the way back to his ranch house and locking the door, maybe even putting a restraining order out on her, not grinning. Maybe Norma put some kind of pixie dust in the strawberry jam he ate on everything but tacos. Or maybe the last jar had fermented and he was really loopy from eating it.

"Good time of the year to have a baby. Not so hot and the hard winter is over," he said.

She looked at him again. "What is the matter with you?"

He ignored the question and went on. "I was determined not to like any of you, but you aren't what I thought you would be. I guess Norma and Hannah had their reasons for not ever visiting each other."

"What did you think they were?"

He settled her into the passenger's seat and circled around the back of the truck. When he was buckled up and driving past the fruit stand he answered, "I thought y'all were too highfalutin and hoity-toity to come to a place like Emet and visit her."

"What?" she yelled.

"Hey, don't yell at me."

"I will if I want to. You aren't supposed to think this is all right. You are supposed to run from me, not act like it's the best news in the whole world," she said.

"You going to get a cherry, rainbow, or coconut crème snow cone?" he asked.

"Don't change the subject," she said.

"I will if I want to."

"I swear I'll never understand men. I hope these babies are girls," she huffed.

"Girls. Boys. One of each. Whatever. I'm just glad there are two of them," he said.

"Why?"

"Because a child shouldn't be raised up alone. Now tell me if there's going to be some jam in the fruit stand tomorrow morning. I know Karen has been making it, and Sue said you've sold all that was in the cellar, so Norma's is all gone."

"You are crazy!"

"Maybe. Blame it on the jam."

❖ ❖ ❖

Luke walked her to the door and caged her by putting an arm on either side of her. "Next time we go on a date I'll arrive all cleaned up and smelling good. You are going with me to the fireworks, right?"

"This was a date?" she asked.

"Yes, ma'am. Man takes a woman for a snow cone after a long, hot day, it's a real date," he whispered.

"What if he takes her to the fireworks? Does that mean it's serious?"

"Oh, yes, it does. Knowing that, you will still go with me, right?"

She nodded.

His lips met hers in a long, lingering kiss that made every nerve ending in her body tingle. "I'll pick you up at seven. Don't eat. We'll grab a burger before the fireworks start."

She couldn't say a word. Never had she experienced such a rush over a good-night kiss. She nodded again and he whistled the whole way back to his truck. She willed her jelly-filled knees to carry her into the house, and plopped down on the sofa beside Hannah.

"Nanna, is it wrong to be pregnant with one man's child— or twins, as this case is—and get all mushy feeling when another man kisses you?"

Hannah smiled. "I don't think one has anything to do with the other."

"I still can't believe this summer is happening to any of us. I like Luke a lot, but he's four years older than me, and I'm about to have twins. I just thought things were complicated that day in Morgantown when I did the home pregnancy test. They go way beyond that now. And now I'm the first Brewer woman to have twins. If they're boys I'll know I'm dreaming because Brewers only have one child and they're girls."

Hannah picked up the remote and turned off the television. "You aren't dreaming and you are not the first Brewer to have twins."

"What did you say, Mother?" Karen asked.

"I said she's not the first Brewer woman to have twins," Hannah said. She hadn't planned to tell them the story at ten o'clock at night when they should all be getting a good night's rest for another grueling day in the peaches. But it was time.

"Were you a twin? Did Grandmother have twins?" Karen asked.

"No, I had twins," Hannah said.

"I'm a twin? You never told me that," Karen said.

Hannah shook her head. "No, you are an only child."

Kim looked from one to the other. "Then you had twins after Grandma was born?"

"Well, how about that? A family secret," Sue said.

Hannah smiled. "I guess it is, and it'll take a while to tell. World War II changed things. Women had held down the home front while their men were gone and they were breaking free of the homemaking mold. Men folks were fighting to keep them tightened down. My father fought harder than the rest. What Daddy said was the law and no one crossed him. I was almost seventeen that spring and Daddy and Mother had the annual railroad party out on our lawn. All-day croquet, games, food, and then a dance with a band that evening. One of the railroad engineers brought his son to the party. He was in the military and about to be shipped to Korea where the new battle lines were. Hank was his name and he was home on furlough and Lord, that man was handsome. He was nineteen and his eyes were black and his hair even blacker. He had a dimple in his chin and his kisses set my heart to tingling. I can still see the devil dancing in those dark eyes."

"Nanna!" Kim said.

"I wasn't Nanna then. I was on the brink of womanhood and Hank taught me how much fun kissing could be. Daddy hated him from the first time he laid eyes on him. No way was I dating that wild boy."

"That's like Norma and Ricky," Sue said.

"Exactly! Anyway, we eloped and spent a weekend together before he shipped out. I saw him off on the train out of DC, then I caught a train back home. Mother, Daddy, and a lawyer were waiting in the living room when I got there. It was annulled right then, like yours, Kim. And then I found out I was pregnant. Twins, but I didn't know it then. History repeats itself for sure. I was pregnant and knew Hank would come back someday and we'd get married again as soon as he got home. I got two letters from him before Mother figured out I was pregnant," Hannah said.

"And?" Kim asked.

"Daddy had a distant cousin in Oklahoma and we were on the next train. When the baby was born, his cousin would find a good family to adopt it. The story would be that he'd sent me away for six months to study at a fancy school. Daddy said he'd find me a decent husband when I was old enough to get married."

"So that's why you came to Oklahoma," Sue said.

"Hank didn't come back, did he?" Karen asked.

Hannah shook her head. "Mother and I came to Ravia on a train and Norma's daddy picked us up. We had a private car and Mother hardly spoke to me the whole way. I swore if I ever got off that train I'd never set foot in Morgantown again. I wasn't giving up my baby for adoption, not even if I had to run away. Hank would come home and get me. We'd make a life of our own."

"Go on," Karen said.

"And I met Norma. She was in love with Ricky. I told her I was pregnant and they were going to make me give my baby away. We conjured up one plan after another, which was all just dreams. When her father spoke, Ricky disappeared. When mine did, I was in exile."

"Did you ever hear from Hank again?" Kim asked.

Hannah nodded. "Yes, I did. We'd been here a week when Norma's father went into town and came back with Jesse Brewer. Jesse was the manager of the hotel Daddy had just invested in. It was called The Morgantown Inn back in those days. He couldn't go to war because he'd had rheumatic fever as a child and without his glasses, he was nearly blind. At twenty-two he was a thin little man, wore round spectacles that kept slipping down on his nose, and was a real bookworm type of fellow. I couldn't understand why on earth he was here."

"He snuck you a letter from Hank, didn't he?" Kim asked.

Hannah nodded. "I guess he did at that. Mother told me to go sit on the porch with Jesse and so I did. I thought that Daddy must have died for Jesse to have come that whole way to talk to me. I went outside and all the others stayed in the house."

"Well?" Karen asked.

Hannah inhaled and let it out slowly. "Jesse handed me a letter. Hank had written letters like all the soldiers did in those days to be delivered to his family when he died. He said that if I was reading the letter that he was already gone and he was so sorry he'd never get to see his baby. He'd gotten the letter about the pregnancy the day before and then he said that loving me was the best thing he'd ever done and it had been the best time of his whole life."

"Did you give the baby away? Do I have a sibling some-where?" Karen asked.

Kim hugged Hannah in a fierce squeeze. "I'm so sorry, Nanna."

Hannah looked at Karen. "You, my child, are the only child I had with your father. I was sitting there with a bro-ken heart, pregnant, and Jesse Brewer said he'd been in love with me for months but he wasn't stupid. There was no way my father would ever let him court me. And then Jesse had heard my father talking to a lawyer about the adoption and he offered to marry me. My father said if I married Jesse I could come back home with him and Mother on the train. He would give us the hotel and I could keep my baby."

"But you didn't love him," Kim said.

"No, I didn't. How could I? I'd married the man I loved and he was dead. Jesse said he realized I didn't love him but that I might learn to someday and he'd be willing to give me time. You've got to remember I was seventeen and I'd no experience at anything other than setting the table for supper and helping Mother plan parties. I told Jesse I'd marry him."

"What happened?" Kim asked.

"We got married the next morning."

Karen tilted her head to one side. "And?"

"We had another private car on the way back to Morgantown. Mother and I had the bunk beds. Jesse slept on the couch. When we arrived, Daddy was waiting at the station. He took us to the hotel, where we took up residence in the penthouse apartment. The story was that Daddy sent me away because I'd fallen in love with Jesse, but then he saw how much Jesse loved me so he finally gave his blessing. Jesse came to Oklahoma and we were married and I got pregnant on the honeymoon back to West Virginia. Everyone thought it was so romantic. I went into labor at the seventh month. Twins cause that sometimes. They were born late one night and both of them died before daylight. Boys. Twin boys that looked exactly like their father, down to the clefts in their little chins."

"Oh, Nanna." Tears flowed down Kim's cheeks.

"Brothers," Karen whispered.

"Never thought of it like that, but you're right. It was that night that I fell in love with Jesse. He held one of those little boys in his arms and I held the other one until they both died. He cried as hard as I did and prayed that his sons would live. We had a graveside service. Jesse and me and the preacher. So there's a little white stone at the head of two graves in the Cosby family cemetery, engraved 'Hank and Jesse, born December thirtieth, died December thirty-first.' We started the New Year with nothing but a friendship born in a night of heartache and it grew into a lasting and deep love."

Tears dripped off Karen's cheekbones onto her nightshirt. "Why didn't you ever tell me that story? I thought you were perfect."

Hannah smiled. "Your father thought I was too. And I learned to love him. He was a good man, Karen. Our love was one of those steady things that grew with time. It wasn't a blue flame like I had with Hank, but sometimes that kind of love burns hot then flickers and dies. I'm glad for the years I had with Jesse and he loved you so much."

The clock chimed one time. It was eleven thirty, but no one moved.

"Why'd you tell us?" Kim asked.

"You said you were having twins and didn't know that there were any in the family. Well, darlin', when I get where I'm finally going, I don't want to walk up to those pearly gates with any secrets or unfinished business. Now let's go to bed. Tomorrow is another busy day."

Kim wiped the final tears from her cheeks. "That's why you didn't get all up in arms and judge me when I told y'all I was pregnant. Guess we're the two with a wild streak. These other two are perfect."

Karen stood up. "I'm glad you married my father and I had you two for parents. I'm also glad times have changed so Kim doesn't have to face that kind of decision, but rest assured I am not perfect."

"Don't burst my bubble tonight. Your father and I always thought you had wings and a halo," Hannah said, her heart lighter than it had been in years.

CHAPTER THIRTEEN

"Have a bad night? You've got bags under your eyes," Hannah said.

Karen poured a cup of coffee and carried it to the table. "I did. I kept thinking about that secret."

"It's not a sin to be mad at your mother," Hannah said.

"I stayed with Daniel because I was supposed to be faultless like you, and now I find out that you kept this huge secret."

"To begin, you are going to be sixty, not ninety. And it is not my fault that you stayed with Daniel when you found out about his infidelity. The Brewer name is just a name; it's not a deity. You don't get to blame me for your decisions," Hannah said.

"If we were in Morgantown, I would avoid you for a month, but living here makes that impossible."

"You can get glad in the same britches you got mad in. I'm going to speak my mind and we'll deal with it. It really is hard to avoid problems when you live in the same small house, isn't it?" Hannah sipped her coffee.

Karen made a motion with her hand, accidentally caught the edge of her coffee cup, and sent it flying all over the table, onto her nightshirt, and on the floor.

"Secrets! Why didn't you tell me before last night?" she yelled as she grabbed a roll of paper towels from the counter and began to swipe up the mess.

Hannah pushed her chair back and watched. "Did your grandfather ever tell you about my sons? Did your grandmother? You were out there with them a lot of times. Remember?"

Karen shot her a mean look. "Don't pass the buck. You are my mother."

Hannah's eyes narrowed into slits. "I'm not passing the buck. Open your eyes, child. They didn't tell you because they were ashamed of me. They could hardly bear to be in the same room with me at Christmas when we went for holidays. Jesse was better liked than I was. He was the hero for marrying the Cosby disgrace. I didn't tell you because I didn't want to see the same thing in your eyes I saw in theirs. Anything else we need to discuss?"

"I'm not ashamed. I'm confused more than anything else. I haven't been an angel in my time either."

Hannah laughed. "Ah, at last. You are facing a problem instead of running to your wine cellar and hiding from it. I'd begun to think there was something wrong with you."

Karen glared at her mother. "Wrong with me. I was the perfect child."

"That's what was wrong. Never a cross word or rebellious time."

"I had my rebellion, but you're not going to goad out of me what I did. Not today." Karen blushed.

"Go clean up and pick the rest of the peaches. There's a few stragglers and it's cheap therapy. It won't cost you all those thousands you spent after your trip to Italy that summer."

Kim meandered in from her bedroom. "I heard yelling."

"Yes, you did. Your nanna shouldn't keep secrets," Karen said.

"Do you have any?" Kim teased.

Karen set her jaw and turned her back. She heard Kim giggle when she opened her bedroom door.

"What happened and what's cheap therapy?" Kim asked Hannah.

"I gave her some advice. Eighty-year-old women better have advice to give their children or they're good for nothing but filling up a coffin." Hannah refilled her cup and popped a bagel into the toaster. Fat grams and calories be danged! She was having cream cheese and some of that pepper jelly Norma had canned. She'd think about clogged veins later.

Karen slammed the door to the bedroom and Sue peeked out from around the closet door. "Who spit in your oatmeal this morning? Or maybe I should say who sprayed you down with coffee?"

"My mother and your grandmother. I couldn't sleep all night and we had a fight and how can we stay mad at each other when this house is so small? I should have never sold my house and brought all my stuff to this godforsaken wilderness," Karen huffed.

"Mother, it's normal. Daughters have this flawless character vision of their parents. You and Daddy never had raging hormones and you had sex only one time—to produce me. Nanna had a secret. Get used to it," Sue said.

"This is a dysfunctional family after all. Everyone is just brimming full of advice. And all this time I thought we were all perfect except for me," Karen said.

Sue hugged her. "And I thought the same thing."

Kim waltzed into the room. "I was eavesdropping right outside the door."

"You are terrible," Sue said.

"Blame it on the pregnancy, but after last night, I'm afraid no one will tell me their hidden secrets. I do promise not to eavesdrop on you and John anymore, Momma."

Sue blushed scarlet.

❖ ❖ ❖

Luke showed up at the fruit stand in the middle of the afternoon with an ice chest full of cold soda pop. He set it on the floor between two chairs in the fruit stand, opened it up, and popped the lid on a can of lemonade.

Kim reached for it and asked, "We still on for tonight?"

"Yes, we are. Get all pretty and I'll even take a shower," he teased.

"What if I like you all dusty and dirty with hay in your hair?" she asked.

He combed his hair with his fingers, and several pieces of straw fell into his lap. "Your wish is my command. Eau de Sweat or nice-smellin' cologne?"

"I'll take the latter tonight, sir."

"Then that's what you shall have, my lady. Looks like the peaches are all gone." He nodded toward the shelf.

"For today. Nanna says we might have a few more to sell the rest of this week, but there won't be any for next week. I'm starting to see peaches in my sleep."

"By the time they are all harvested, the apples will be ready and then the pears, and after that, when it gets cold, there will be pecans to pick in the evenings," he said.

"Pecans?"

"Got ten trees that bring in a good cash crop, but Norma always shelled out a hundred pounds to freeze for her own cooking." Luke popped the top on a Coke and guzzled down a third of it before he came up for air.

"Luke, seriously now, when is this complicated bit about twins going to sink into your brain?" Kim asked.

"It already did. I'm not perfect, Kim. I've had relationships and even thought about marriage once, but she wasn't ranchin' material and the relationship died in its sleep when hay season came around. With you, I get three for one. That's even better than the odds you get at the last-minute firecracker stands." Luke grinned.

"I'm serious." Kim looked into his twinkling brown eyes.

"So am I, Kim. I know you are pregnant. That doesn't bother me. I like you. I want to date you. That's about as honest as I can get."

"I like you too. That's about as honest as I can get. I'm looking forward to the fireworks thing," she said.

"Then I'll pick you up at seven and we'll get a burger before the fireworks begin."

A few minutes after five, she rushed into the house to get ready to go to Tishomingo. She was already partway down the hall when her brain kicked into gear and she realized what she'd seen in the living room: Hannah was on the sofa with a wet washcloth stretched out over her face and she wasn't moving. Kim turned so fast that she had to brace herself against the wall and ran back to the living room.

"Nanna, are you all right?" she asked.

"I felt pretty weak, but I'm better now. Guess it's time to fess up, but don't tell your mother or Karen. On the Friday before Norma died, my doctor said I needed this surgery to blow out the veins in my neck. I told him I was almost eighty years old and I wasn't having any of it."

Kim sat down hard. "Yes, you will."

"I'd decided to spend my last days here with you all and then go on peacefully, but now I want to live to see the babies," Hannah said.

"I'm calling a doctor tomorrow morning, Nanna. You will have this done and I will tell Momma," Kim said.

"Tell me what?" Sue asked from the back door.

Kim tattled.

Sue set the bushel of peaches on the table and sat down on the sofa arm beside her grandmother. "Yes, you will have it done."

"You don't get to tell me what to do," Hannah said.

"Tell who what?" Karen came up out of the cellar.

Sue tattled.

"Yes, you will! Do we need to go to the emergency room tonight? You are just full of secrets, aren't you?"

"Stop it!" Hannah said. "I'll see Norma's doctor as soon as he can get me in. Edith says he's the best in the area. Kim can call him tomorrow morning, but right now you are all going to go on and let me breathe. You're smothering me to death."

"You need a good specialist. Maybe in Dallas or Oklahoma City," Karen protested.

"I said I'll see Norma's doctor. If he's got a good air pump and a Coke straw, he can do the surgery. When it's all said and done, I'll either live or I won't. Gravity can hold me down here in Emet, or the angels can send Norma to take me on to stroll around heaven with her. I'd like to stay awhile longer, but if I drop in the next thirty seconds, I've never been happier, so it's no big deal. I'm not going to the doctor until tomorrow, and that's final. And Sue and Kim, y'all are staying right here and running the farm as usual. Karen can go with me."

❖ ❖ ❖

Luke knocked on the kitchen door, didn't wait for an answer, and went right in. Kim waited in the middle of the floor wearing a pink sundress and sandals. His breath caught in his chest and he felt as if he would drown before he could inhale again.

"You are beautiful," he said.

"Well, thank you. You like it? Am I too dressed up?" She swirled around, the skirt billowing out.

"No, ma'am. But I'll have to carry a big stick to fend off the other guys tonight. It'll be a fight to the death."

"My knight in shining armor," Kim teased. "Where's the big white horse?"

He crooked his arm. "It's outside. Has Ford written on the side instead of a saddle on its back, but it's what knights ride in this part of the world. Shall we?"

She laced her arm through it. "You don't look so bad yourself, Sir Luke. That's a pretty nice shining denim armor you got on."

"Thank you, my lady." He chuckled.

Luke and Kim had barely disappeared down the road, a cloud of dust trailing behind them, when John's truck crunched the gravel. Sue opened the door before he knocked. He was freshly shaven and water droplets still hung on his hair.

"If the boys fighting over in the Middle East could see you, they'd know their efforts were worthwhile," John said.

"What's that mean?" Sue asked.

"It means that you look beautiful and they'd all agree with me. You look like apple pie, home, and freedom all mixed up together. Some of them would see sexy; others would see peace and home." He took her hand in his and led her to the truck.

"Thank you, I think," she said.

He stepped back and motioned for her to slide into the truck and under the steering wheel. She stopped midway on the wide bench seat, sitting beside him, their thighs touching as he drove toward town.

"I feel like a teenager sitting in the middle like this," she said.

"You're prettier than a teenager. Maturity becomes you."

"Thank you again, I think." She smiled.

"I mean it. Teenagers lack the grace that a mature woman has, but I wish I'd known you all your life, Sue." John threw his arm around her. "And then again, I'm glad our paths are just now crossing because I like you just the way you are now."

"And I like you just the way you are," she whispered.

Hannah was sitting at the kitchen table eating a piece of strawberry shortcake when Karen poured two cups of coffee and sat down at the table. "Where's Sue?"

"She and Kim had dates. Guess we're too old for them," Hannah answered.

"Well, thank God. I'm not in the mood for a bunch of fireworks or for a crowd of people in a football stadium. Let's play a game of Yahtzee, Mother."

Hannah smiled. "Get it out and pour us some lemonade."

CHAPTER FOURTEEN

Kim awoke and reached for Luke, but all she got was an armful of soft pillow. She opened her eyes and moaned. She'd been dreaming about him a lot lately and waking up thinking he was beside her. She threw back the sheet and padded to the kitchen in her bare feet. The sun wasn't even up yet, and in Morgantown she sure wouldn't have been awake at that hour of the morning. And for sure not without an alarm clock. She nodded at her grandmother, made a cup of hot chocolate in the microwave, and carried it to the table.

"So how'd it go with Luke last night?" Hannah asked.

"Great! I met some of his friends. Josh and Crystal. They own a greenhouse over there in Tishomingo, and they've got three cute little girls: Malee, Tess, and Emma. I liked Crystal and she invited me to have lunch with her sometime. Said it'd have to be a day when her mother could watch the girls, so we'd have to plan ahead. Norma ever mention a lady named Trudy? That's Crystal's mother."

"No, she never did, but I'm glad you found a friend. Fireworks pretty?"

"Oh, yeah, and the burgers were good, and Luke kissed me good night at the door. I felt like a princess," Kim said.

"You should. You are a princess," Hannah told her.

"Well, thank you, Nanna! Where's Momma? She's usually up and figuring out some new way to make peaches before I get up."

"She left for the peach orchard to gather up the culls. She's found something called peach chutney that she's dying to try, and there's very few peaches left."

Both of them jumped when the doorbell rang.

"Come in!" Hannah yelled. "It's early for Edith and the girls, but those three get up with the chickens."

The doorbell rang again.

"Guess they didn't get up that early this morning." Kim pushed her chocolate back and opened the door to find her grandfather, Daniel, on the other side. He wore a pale gray suit with a deeper gray shirt and red tie.

She stood back and motioned him inside. "Grandpa, come in. You look horrible. Is something wrong?"

"I need to talk to your grandmother," he said.

"She's out gathering peaches, but she'll be back in a little while. Are you sure you're not sick or..." Kim asked.

"I'll take a cup of coffee. Two sugars and lots of cream," Daniel said without answering her questions. He sat down on the sofa and nodded toward Hannah.

"Daniel," she said seriously. "Really now, what are you doing here?"

"I'll talk to Karen. What I have to say is her business and mine, not yours," Daniel said brusquely.

"Well, she'll tell us anyway." Kim put his cup on a saucer and carried it to him. "We tell each other everything. I was just telling Nanna about my date with Luke."

"Is Luke the father of the baby?"

"No, Luke is my *new* boyfriend. My last boyfriend is the father of my child."

Hannah propped her feet up on one of the other chairs. It was working up to be a good morning after all. Dang it, but she wished Edith and the girls were there to share it. Real life sure beat soap operas. Television could never air the real thing. No one would ever believe it.

"Don't you talk down to me, young lady! It's not too late to fix it even yet. I'll write the check for it," he said.

"Take the check, roll it into a tube, and choke to death on it, Grandpa," Kim said coldly.

Sue was already into the kitchen when she realized she'd just seen her father in the living room. She shook her head, trying to rid herself of the ridiculous vision. Why would he be in Emet again?

Taking five steps backward, she leaned around the door-jamb and looked again. It really was Daniel Tarleton sitting there drinking coffee.

"What's he doing here?" she whispered to Hannah.

"Wants to talk to Karen and it *don't* concern us. He did offer to write a check to pay a doctor to fix Kim's problem."

Sue popped her hands on her hips and glared at her father. "You had the nerve to say that to my child?"

"No 'Hello, Daddy'? No 'How's things going with you, Daddy?' Just walk in here with an attitude and start in on me about something you know would be the right thing to do."

"That's right. Now why are you here?" Sue asked.

"To see your mother. Not you. Not your wayward child. *Your mother.* Go tell her I'm here."

"My mother is in the peach orchard and I'm not disturbing her," Sue said. "You might have a long wait, Daddy dear."

"I'll wait." He tilted his arrogant chin a little farther toward the ceiling.

"Have it your way," Sue said.

She grabbed a handful of cookies, picked her straw hat off the nail, and headed out to the field to give her mother a heads-up about her father. She'd gone only a few steps in that direction when she saw Karen on her way back toward the house, toting a bushel of peaches.

"Hey, you! I didn't think I'd find half this many on the ground, but I think there'll be plenty to make that peach chutney," Karen said.

Sue grabbed the handle on the side of the basket and they carried it between them the rest of the way. "Daddy is in the house acting like God. Telling Kim he'll pay for an abortion. I don't know what he wants, but he wouldn't have taken a red-eye flight and gotten here this early for nothing, and he won't talk to anyone but you."

"He's ticked because I made him buy the house," Karen said. "He's going to try to sweet-talk me into changing my mind one more time before the absolute final papers are signed."

Karen waltzed into the foyer and ignored Daniel. She poured herself a cup of coffee and sat down at the table with Kim and Hannah. "You had your coffee, Sue?"

"Not yet."

"Go ahead and get it, and then we'll talk to your father."

Daniel stormed into the kitchen. "What in the devil are you trying to prove? I was waiting in the living room and I want to talk to you privately, Karen. Without an audience."

"You got something to say, then say it. Right here. When I get finished with my coffee, we're going to peel peaches. Take off your coat and roll up your sleeves if you plan on staying, because anybody that don't work here, don't eat," she said.

"You don't belong here doing manual labor like that, and you look horrible. Let's take a drive and talk," he said through clenched teeth.

"My terms are that I'll listen to what you have to say while I have my morning coffee," she said.

"Why are you being so difficult? We have a wonderful home, good friends, and a great life." His voice changed from cold to sickening sweet in an instant.

"That won't work anymore," she said. "Sit down or get out."

"Have it your way." He went to the table and pulled out a chair for her.

"Thank you," she said formally.

"Please come home." He picked up her hand and kissed her fingertips.

"Why would I do that? I'm sure Tiffany is much more comfortable with me completely out of the picture. I think your words were that I was a threat to her and did I remember what it was like to be young and in love?"

Daniel kissed them again, one by one, lingering over them as if he was eating a five-course meal with each one. "We can fly to Italy. We'll get remarried in that big hotel. I'll even spring for a new diamond wedding ring. This time with a stone so big it'll look like a chunk of an ice-skating rink. All the women at the country club will be envious."

Karen pulled her hand away and wiped it on the legs of her overalls. "Tiffany left you, did she?"

Daniel nodded. "She said I'd promised her a big house just like she wanted and if she couldn't have it the wedding was off. I told her that it had taken most of my resources to buy you out so she wouldn't have to worry about you being around. The plantation house could be refurnished any way she wanted."

"And she refused?" Kim asked.

Another nod. "She is gone from my life forever. I'm so sorry, Karen. I didn't realize what I was losing, and I'm an idiot for the way I've acted. I can't live without you. I'll never cheat on you again. God can strike me dead on the spot if I do. Please come home. I need you. I can't make the winery work without you. I've been a fool."

Hannah held her breath.

Karen laid a hand on his shoulder.

Hannah almost wept.

Karen leaned forward and said, "Yes, you have been a fool, Daniel. There comes a time in everyone's life when it's too late to do what you should have been doing all along. I'm not going to marry you. You are an intelligent man and you can run the winery. And another thing, it's time to make amends with your daughter for whatever you two have been fighting about for more than twenty years. Learn to love your granddaughter. Be a good great-grandfather to those twins Kim is carrying. You can have a full life even at your age. But I'm not going to be a part of it."

"You're sure? I love you. We could still be good together. I'll do what you said if you'll come home. I'll be friends with Sue and Kim, if you marry me. No promises if you don't," he said through clenched teeth.

"That's your loss if you don't. They're pretty amazing women. I'm getting to know them and my mother really well," Karen said.

Daniel stood up slowly, ran his fingers through his hair. "When I walk out the door, the offer is off the table. Want to think about it?"

"Don't let the door hit you in the hind end on the way out," Karen said.

Hannah exhaled so loudly the other three women jumped to make sure she hadn't had a fatal heart attack.

He slung gravel all over the porch when he peeled out of the driveway.

"Remind me to have that driveway paved when the harvest is done," Karen said cheerfully.

CHAPTER FIFTEEN

The sun was just setting. The last load of the peaches had been picked. A big round outdoor thermometer attached to the nearest tree in the backyard declared that it was still ninety-eight degrees. The clock on the mantel struck eight times. No one moved except to take another drink of lemonade and sigh occasionally.

"Is it really finished?" Kim asked. "Is every last peach picked, canned, and put away?"

Karen sighed. "And now apples! Hey, I've been thinking about putting some quick breads at the fruit stand for fall. Maybe cranberry, apple cinnamon, and orange slice. What do y'all think?" Karen asked.

"Of course they'll sell. I figured you'd be reconsidering Daddy's offer after the peaches," Sue said.

Kim sipped lemonade. "Why did you stay with him, Grandma?"

"Because she was a southern lady who didn't admit defeat," Hannah answered.

Karen shrugged. "Wrong is wrong. Don't matter if it's one time or a dozen or more. It was the same. Quantity doesn't mean anything when it comes to sin. I wasn't a bit better than he was."

"You?" Kim gasped.

Karen looked at Sue. "Remember that summer when I went to Italy alone?"

"I won't ever forget that summer." Sue's eyes widened when she realized what her mother was saying. "You didn't, did you?"

"Your father and I had another big fight and the Italian wine tour came up. He was supposed to go but I set my foot down and said he could stay home with you for once and I didn't even care if he cheated the whole time I was gone. I left on a bad note and when I got to Italy, I was so angry that I didn't even plan to come back home. I met a widower with his own vineyard. I came home to file for a divorce."

"Why didn't you?" Sue asked.

"You were withdrawn. Your father was suddenly attentive, admitting he'd been a bad boy in the past but he'd never cheat again. Swore on his dead mother's name and offered to bring out the Bible. I believe it lasted a week before he was flirting with some sweet young blonde at the next party we attended. Basically, I'm no better than he is."

"I disagree," Hannah said. "But now I understand why you stayed with him. You became your own whipping tree."

Karen shrugged again. "I didn't realize it at the time, but it's what I did. If we'd been in Morgantown when Tiffany left him, I would have probably let him sweet-talk me into staying again."

Hannah held her glass up in the air. "Then thank you, Norma."

Sue's blue eyes narrowed into slits. "Why didn't you leave him? You just left an example for me to be a martyr just like you. If you would have taken me to Italy, I might...I don't even know how to say this."

"Believe it or not, I know just how you feel," Karen said.

Sue shook her head. "How could you?"

"Because I felt the same way after Mother told us about the twins. If she had been honest then I wouldn't have felt like I had to be the faultless daughter. If I'd known she wasn't some kind of pure saint, I wouldn't have had to live up to her example."

Kim sat her glass down with a thud on the coffee table. "Oh, all of you hush! If Nanna hadn't kept her secret, you might have left Granddad and gone to Italy. If that would have happened, Mother would have never married my father and there would be no me. So I'm glad you stayed with him. Not that I want you to go back to Morgantown now. We've all become a family rather than just a bunch of women who share a bloodline."

"Out of the mouths of babes," Hannah intoned.

"I still have the right to be upset," Sue said.

"You have that right." Karen slung an arm around her daughter. "I'm actually glad to see you showing emotion again. Does John bring that out in you? If so, I hope he never leaves us."

"This place brings that out in me," Sue said. "That and living like sardines with the three of you in this little house. I can't cuss a cat without getting a hair in my mouth. I think I'm going to take the money from the sale of my house and build a new place of my own. Not far, just over in that pasture—if I can talk John into selling me an acre."

"Aha," Kim said. "So Grandma is talking about building her own place pretty soon and you're going to build one.

Nanna can live here and I'll move in with Luke. We'll all still be close but not cramped up like sardines."

Sue whipped around to face Kim. "You will what?"

Kim giggled. "I get weak knees every time I see him. He feels the same about me and it's what people do these days. They live together before they commit to a marriage. If I'd lived with Marshall a week we wouldn't have had to get an annulment."

"But," Sue stammered.

"I thought you two argue too much to live together," Hannah said.

"We speak our minds, but that doesn't mean I'm not going to wind up with him," Kim said.

"You are pregnant," Sue reminded her.

"That's right. Pregnant with twins. Not dead. Not blind. Loosen up, Momma. Have you kissed John? If not, you'd better at the barbecue tomorrow night because I bet there's going to be a bunch of pretty women there who'd take him away from you in a heartbeat. And I was just teasing about living with Luke. I want the whole forever thing, and I'm willing to wait for it."

John's barbecue was an event in Emet that happened every year just before school started. Everyone in the community was invited and usually showed up. It was held between the house and bunkhouse, and there was always a live band for dancing, lots of smoked brisket, turkey, pork loin, and visiting. It was a BYOLC—bring your own lawn chair—affair that the whole community looked forward to all summer.

John hadn't even realized the Brewer women had arrived until he looked across the lawn and saw Sue sitting in front of the bandstand. He brought a chair over and sat down. His hand reached over and took hers, and he kissed her on the cheek. "Having a good time? I didn't see y'all coming in."

"It's kind of like the dinner after that first Sunday, only there's music," she said.

"Get-togethers around here are like that," he said. "Want to dance?"

She stood up and he led her out to the middle of the yard. The band's lead singer started an old George Jones tune, "I Cross My Heart." Sue listened to the lyrics with one ear and to John's steady heartbeat with the other as they two-stepped. How it had happened in one summer was a mystery, but living in Emet felt right, her relationship with John felt right, and the camaraderie with her family felt right.

"When are you going back to West Virginia to get things settled with that house business?" John asked.

Sue looked up at him. "Mother made a clean break. I think that's what I'll do too. I was amazed when my house sold the first week it was on the market, and the new owners—also teachers—want to take possession immediately. So I hired packers to take care of it all and movers to bring it to the storage unit where Mother has her things. I'd like to build a house of my own. Nothing big or fancy, but something that is mine. Nanna can have Norma's house."

"I see. And where do you want to put this house?" John asked.

"In your pasture. I like that little bunch of trees across the lane from Nanna's house, and I'd like to build right there. Want to sell me an acre?" Sue smiled.

"Maybe I could be coerced. Six Friday-night dates and we'll talk about it," he said.

"But you already come to our house on Friday night and Nanna looks forward to those nights," she countered.

"Then Saturday night for six weeks. We'll go out. To dinner. To a movie. Just the two of us." He held his breath.

"Deal. Six of them and you'll sell me an acre." She nodded.

"Six and we'll talk about the sale," he said.

"Still a deal." A grin tickled the corners of her mouth.

Someone tapped Sue on the shoulder, and she looked around, expecting to see another cowboy wanting to cut into the dance. But it was Luke, wearing an apron with a big fat pink pig on the front.

"Where is Kim?" he asked.

"Looking for you," Sue said.

"I'm right here." Kim peeked around John's arm.

"Well, come on, woman. I'm cookin' and you're helping me," he said.

John chuckled. "Children!"

"Ever want any?" Sue asked.

"Luke is as good as my son, but I wouldn't mind having a dozen," he said.

Sue's heart fell. She was almost forty years old. She sure didn't have time to produce a dozen kids, and besides, she'd never had any more after Kim was born.

"But," John went on, "if you'll let me share your grandkids, I could be happy with that."

❖ ❖ ❖

"What am I supposed to do?" Kim asked.

"Keep the table. That means keep plenty of plates and forks out and smile pretty when the folks come through to fill up their plates. Only the most beautiful woman in the county gets to do that job. There is your throne, Princess." Luke pointed to a lawn chair.

"Princess? I thought I was the queen of the barbecue," she said.

"Not as long as Hannah is alive. I missed you," he said.

"Me too. You haven't even been to the fruit stand in three days," she told him.

"Had to finish the hay, get ready for the party, and plow up a couple of fields. School starts in two weeks," he said.

"Momma said tonight she's going to build her own house. She says she's buying an acre of John's pasture to put it on," Kim told him.

"John wouldn't give up two feet of that pasture. He's worked his whole life for that land," Luke said.

Kim picked up a plate and handed it to Edith. "Try that pork stuff. I had a bite and it's really good."

"Oh, honey, I know it. I wouldn't miss this barbecue for nothing. I saw one of your momma's lemon cakes over there. I'm going to get a slice before it's all gone. See you later," she said.

"Kim, I mean it. John won't sell a foot of his land," Luke whispered.

"Ever seen the way he looks at her? I bet she gets it."

"Want to put a wager on it? You might beat me at the pool table, but I know John. That land is like God to him."

"How much?"

"I get to name one of the twins if she gets the land."

"And if she doesn't?"

"I get to name the other one." He laughed.

She poked him in the arm with the plastic fork. Two tines broke when they struck his rock-hard muscles. "How about if she gets the land, then you owe me a steak dinner?"

"And if she doesn't, you'll marry me. That'll give them more room in the house."

"Don't tease me. If she doesn't get the land you have to buy me all the catfish I can eat at Fish Tales, and, honey, I'm eating for three, so don't think you'll be getting off cheap," Kim told him.

"Deal." He wiped his hand on his jeans and held it out.

They shook hands and he pulled her into an embrace. "I wasn't teasing."

She looked up into his eyes. "I know, but it's too soon, Luke."

He leaned across a foot of hot summer night and kissed her softly. "Some things are just there, Kim, and when they are, it's right."

"Marriage is a big step, Luke," she whispered.

"Yes, it is. There comes Hannah and Myrtle. It's time for the princess to earn her crown," he said.

"Ah, shucks. I thought you'd kiss me again in front of the whole bunch of people so they'd know that you're a knight in shining pig apron and I am the princess of the plastic plates and never the two will be parted."

Luke laughed. "You are a witch, woman."

"Yes, I am, and I come from a long line of witches, so you'd better rethink that proposal. Nanna burns black candles and does chants at night."

Luke laughed again. "Go do your duties, and when this next batch gets done, we'll dance."

"You dance and cook too?" she asked.

"I'm full of surprises, Princess Plastic Plate!"

Half an hour later, Luke led Kim out into the yard. He put his arms around her and pulled her close, burying his nose in the sweet smell of her hair. The song was little more than halfway finished and Kim's eyes were shut when someone tapped on her shoulder.

"Mind if I cut in?"

Her eyelids snapped open to see a tall, dark-haired girl with doe-colored eyes smiling at her elbow. Not looking at her but at Luke, as if she could lay him out naked on a silver platter and have him for breakfast.

"Tambra?" he said.

Kim stepped back. "Be my guest. Be careful, though. He's a bit clumsy with that left foot," Kim said. She hoped the darkness covered the greenish cast in her face as she headed over to where Hannah and her three bosom buddies had their heads together, whispering.

"You all gossiping?" Kim asked.

Hannah patted a chair beside her. "Sit down and talk to us. Why did you let that hussy cut into your dance?"

"What're you going to do about that?" Edith asked.

"About what?" Kim asked right back.

"You going to let that woman take your man?" Myrtle piped up.

"Emet hasn't got many bachelors. Luke is at the top of a short list. Teacher with a solid job. Tambra has had her eye set on him for a long time, but he's been running hard," Virgie said.

"So what are you going to do? Fight or stand down?" Hannah asked.

There was no doubt that the ladies were telling her the gospel truth. Tambra was looking up at him and smiling. Her hand was crooked around his neck and her fingers toyed with his hair.

"Guess that's about enough," Kim said when the song ended.

"If it's worth having, it's worth fighting for," Edith said.

Kim went back out to the middle of the yard. She extended her hand to Tambra, who had to let go of Luke's to shake with her.

"I don't think we've met. I'm Kim DeHaven. Hannah's granddaughter. We inherited Norma's farm and orchard this summer. You live around here?"

"Tambra Torres. I'm pleased to meet you. If you'll excuse me, I've called this dance too." She tried to pull her hand back but Kim held on, squeezing tighter.

"Luke, darlin', would you be so kind as to get me a bottle of cold water? I'm just about dried out. Must be the heat. We'll be over there on your pickup tailgate," Kim said.

"Sure, but…" Luke stammered.

"Tambra and I'll visit a few minutes, and then you and I'll have to get back to our duties." Kim smiled.

Luke nodded and headed toward the tub filled with ice, water, and soft drinks at the end of the food table.

"Back off," Tambra hissed. "If you think for one minute you're going to come into my town and harvest my crop, you have sand for brains, woman. Luke is mine and has been since we were kids."

"Has he proposed to you?"

"No, but he will."

"I don't think so, honey," Kim said.

"I'll ruin this party if I start a fight. I'm a country girl and you don't have a chance against me," Tambra said.

"I don't doubt it. Why didn't you come around to Norma's funeral?" Kim asked.

"I was in Texas working on a ranch through the summer months. I just got back. What's that got to do with anything?"

"I didn't think I'd seen you around here. I run the fruit stand, so I've met most everyone in Emet and a lot of the folks from Milburn and Nida." Kim continued to lead the way toward Luke's truck.

Tambra popped her fists on her hips. "Stop right there. We're out far enough from the crowd now that we won't disturb the party. Luke is mine and you're going to back off and leave him alone. No more dancing that close. Do you understand me?"

Her waist was small. Her jeans tight. Her bosom high and running Dolly Parton competition. She was definitely bigger and meaner than Kim.

Whatever's worth having is worth fighting for.

"I'm pregnant," Kim said.

Tambra stared, slack-jawed.

"With twins. Do we understand each other?" Kim asked.

"You won fair and square. I'll leave him alone. He'll just have to be content with second-best." Tambra flounced back to the party.

"You get to know her?" Luke appeared at her elbow with a bottle of water in his hand.

"I think we got to know each other very well. Tambra and I had a little business, but it's taken care of. Want to dance? I think you owe me a full dance before we go back to the food table."

Luke led her out to the dance area again. "Now tell me what happened."

She melted into his arms. "Had to wage a major war, but anything worth having is worth fighting for—Nanna and her friends' words, not mine."

"Who won and what was the prize?" He leaned back to look at her closer.

"I won. I don't play or fight fair. You have been warned."

"And what was the prize?"

"You." She pulled his lips down for a kiss right there in front of everyone—her Nanna, grandmother, mother, Edith, John, the hired help, Tambra, and even God.

CHAPTER SIXTEEN

Kim paced from the door to the back of the waiting room, from there out into the hospital hallway. Luke held her hand and made every step with her. Hannah had been in the surgery for twenty minutes, but it seemed like twenty hours.

Sue leafed through a magazine without seeing a thing. Not even the recipes slowed her methodical page-turning. John threw an arm around her shoulders and patted her arm.

New people came into the room, but Karen didn't even look up from her book. Several had come and gone, and it would be a while before the doctor finished the surgery. So when Edith sat down beside her and touched her on the arm she jumped.

"Didn't mean to scare you," Edith said.

"I wasn't expecting you ladies." Karen put the book inside her purse.

All three lined up in the chairs beside Sue. "We thought we'd come on down here and keep y'all company while you was waitin'. Sometimes it's a long time on this side of the surgery business. Now on the other side, where Hannah is, one minute they tell you to count backward and the next you are wakin' up all groggy."

The lady wearing a purple volunteer smock behind the desk called out, "Logan. Family of Logan. Follow me, please, and the doctor will visit with you."

"Your name will get called pretty soon," Edith said. "Time don't run right in here. The clocks are slow as molasses in December, I'm here to tell you."

"Now you know how we felt," Myrtle said.

"Worried about you the whole time," Virgie admitted.

"You had this done?" Sue asked.

"Oh, yeah. About ten years ago. Doctor said either blow 'em out or pick out a casket. I went down to the funeral home and looked at the caskets, but not a one of them looked comfortable, so I had the surgery," Edith teased.

Sue smiled. "You are a bad influence on Nanna."

"Me? I don't think so, darlin'. She's another Norma, and that woman taught me how to be ornery."

Virgie cut her eyes around at Edith. "Don't be blamin' the dead or Hannah for your wild streak. You've had that since birth."

Myrtle shook her head. "You both have horns instead of a pretty halo like I've got."

"Hmmmph," Virgie snorted. "If that bit of fluff under your hair is a halo somebody made a big mistake. You are the biggest troublemaker among us. Norma never could straighten you out. Why, I could tell you stories on this woman that would curl your toenails."

"Oh, yeah?" Kim caught the last of the conversation and drew up a chair to face the ladies.

Luke did the same and slung an arm over the back of Kim's chair. "We could use a good story."

The volunteer lady said, "Brannon? Family of Brannon, follow me, please. The doctor will visit with you in here," and off went a man and woman trailing behind her as if she were holding the keys to the Pearly Gates.

"I thought she was going to say Brewer," Sue said.

"You'll be next," Edith said.

"How do you know that?" Kim asked.

"Because I been in here often enough to know the way of things," Edith answered.

"And because you three and Hannah aren't going to tell stories, are you?" Karen asked.

"Now you are gettin' smart. We aren't so old that we don't remember, but if we told you," Myrtle leaned forward and whispered, "then we'd have to…"

"Kill us." Kim finally smiled.

"Oh, no, honey, then we'd have to initiate you into the club," Virgie teased.

"And what do I have to do to get initiated?" Kim played along.

"Well, it's a long, drawn-out process that we do not ever discuss in front of menfolk," Virgie said.

John and Luke put on fake hurt expressions.

"Sorry, boys, it's the rules," Edith said.

"It's sexist," Luke said.

"Well, you are sexy, the both of you, but what has that got to do with anything?" Edith asked.

"Sexist, as in you cannot discriminate and keep boys out of your club," Luke argued.

"Honey, when you are eighty you can do anything you darn well please," Myrtle told him.

Virgie checked her watch. "It's about time."

The woman marked out a name on the list in front of her and said, "Brewer? Family for Brewer. Follow me, please. The doctor will talk to you in here."

They marched like little wind-up toys behind the purple smock into a pink waiting room. The pink walls were divided with a six-inch border of a pastoral scene with cows and houses. It looked like Ireland with the pinks and purples in the sun as it set over the rolling hills of green dividing the walls.

Edith motioned toward it as they sat down. "Some psychology person probably said that was to calm us all down while we wait on the doctor. Think about green pastures and cows. Don't calm me down much. Makes me think about all the years me and my husband ran a dairy and milked twice a day. Nothing calm about that."

"Or how about those houses with that ivy all growing up on them." Virgie pointed. "I planted English ivy out in front of my house one year and the danged stuff started creeping up the house. Remember how pretty I thought it was until Norma reminded me of what it had done to her smokehouse? While they were tiny, the vines crept into the crevices between the sheet metal and then wrapped themselves around the studs and pretty soon it was an unholy mess."

The doctor came in, his face mask hanging around his neck like a cowboy's sweaty old bandanna after a hard day's work. He pulled a chair across the floor and sat in the middle of the eight-people circle.

"Everything went fine. She will be in recovery in an hour. You can see her then. Two at a time for five minutes only. After she's lucid, we'll move her to a private room, and she'll be there until day after tomorrow. There was massive blockage in the veins, and she was a walking heart attack or stroke. We'll see her in my office in a week, then in six weeks after that. Any questions?" The doctor asked.

Karen held up a finger. "Just one? She's been talking about a cruise this fall. Do you think that would be wise?"

"Oh, yes." The young doctor smiled. "If my grandmother was like Mrs. Brewer, I'd give her my blessings. She's got grit. By the time she gets back from the cruise she may want to take up belly dancing. And yes, I'll tell her that's fine too. But not for six weeks. After that she'll need to follow a heart-healthy diet, get regular checkups, and see me once a year."

"Thank you." Karen smiled.

Edith turned to the others when the doctor was gone and said, "Belly dancing. Hadn't thought of that. Reckon she'd want some company?"

❖ ❖ ❖

Hannah opened her eyes to see her mother leaning over the bed. Was the baby a boy or a girl? Where was Jesse? He'd been right beside her when they had moved her bed across the hall to the birthing room.

"Is the baby all right?" Hannah asked.

"Of course," Karen said.

The next time her eyes fluttered another woman leaned over the rails of the bed. She said something that sounded like "Hannah," but not exactly. Hannah forced her eyes open long enough to see the woman through the fog and realized it wasn't a nurse.

"Is it all right? It was born too early, you know," Hannah muttered.

"Nanna, who was born too early?" Sue asked.

"Where is Jesse?" Hannah asked in the most authoritative voice she could muster.

"He's been gone for years," Sue said.

"No, he's not. He's across the hall." She shut her eyes tightly and let the fog wash back over her like a warm blanket.

When she opened them the third time, Kim and Luke were sitting beside her bed. Off-white curtains sectioned off her bed on three sides. All kinds of equipment filled up the space to her right. Kim and Luke were deep in conversation to her left.

"I lived through it," she said.

Her nurse leaned over the bed. "Of course you lived. You're a spunky old gal."

"Yes, I am," Hannah said clearly.

Kim jumped up and kissed her on the forehead. "Nanna, how do you feel?"

"I want a drink. Sweet tea," she rasped.

"Ice chips," the nurse said. "For several hours yet."

Kim spooned a few chips into Hannah's mouth and she opened her mouth for more.

"I can go on a cruise. Doctor said so." Her eyes snapped shut and she slept again.

Kim stared at the nurse. "I thought she was awake."

"It happens. She'll drift in and out most of today. By tomorrow she'll want to go dancing," Sally said.

"How long will she sleep this time?" Luke asked.

"Maybe ten minutes. Maybe an hour. She won't even remember this part. She'll wake up for absolute real in a couple of hours."

When Hannah awoke the next time, Edith and Virgie were beside the bed. "Well, I am alive. Y'all ready for a cruise?"

"Sure, anytime you are. Is the whole family going?" Virgie laughed.

"You said stuff like that when you were waking up." Myrtle poked Edith on the arm.

Hannah cut her eyes around at Myrtle. "I'm serious. And none of my family is going. Just us four are going."

"Of course we are," Virgie indulged her. "I won the lottery last week. I can afford it."

"Y'all aren't paying a dime. It's on me because I made a bucket list to do if I wake up, and by golly, I don't want to go by myself. And you've helped me all summer, so you deserve some fun. Have you seen Jesse?" She faded out again.

"Was I that goofy?" Edith asked.

"Yes, you were. In both of your surgeries. You were worse when they did the gallbladder thing. I thought we'd have to go dig up your husband to prove he was dead and not in the room with you," Virgie told her.

Edith reached through the rails and held Hannah's hand. "I bet I didn't talk about a cruise. Lord, that would cost a fortune. We'll have to tease her about it when she gets home. Hey, my oldest boy has got one of them pontoon boats he takes down to the river when it's deep enough to run it. We could get him to take us all fishing and tell her we're taking our cruise."

"Sounds like a plan to me," Virgie said.

Hannah opened her eyes. "We'll each have our own room on the ship. Never know what kind of saggy butt we might find," she said and drifted off again.

She snored through the move to the room on the next floor. When she opened her eyes again, she was lucid.

"I lived. Is it over? What did the doctor say?" she asked.

All six women surrounded her bed.

Karen took the lead. "He said your arteries were blocked severely but he put a straw in there and blew them out and you can go home day after tomorrow. And that you can go on the cruise."

"Good! I was going whether or not he said I could."

The doctor pushed into the room. "Is that right?"

"I'm eighty. You take care of my heart and I'll take care of my life."

"Spicy, isn't she?" He chuckled.

"You don't know the half of it," Kim said.

"If I could get someone to bring me something that wasn't split down the back and some shoes, I'd blow this joint and stop at a steak house to eat on my way home. Don't reckon any of y'all would do that for me, would you?" Hannah looked from one face to the next.

"Nanna!" Sue giggled.

Hannah narrowed her eyes at the doctor. "Day after tomorrow or I'll do it. I told you, I have a cruise to plan. I can't be wallowing around in a bed forever. You said everything went fine. I want to get back home and take care of business."

"You can. First thing, day after tomorrow. By then you'll be so feisty that I'll kick you out of here and give your bed to someone who's really sick," he said.

"I can live with that," she said. "When can I have something to eat?"

"Supper will be served in an hour. Jell-O, broth, apple juice," the doctor answered.

"Yum, yum," Hannah said sarcastically.

"And a heart-healthy diet from now on. Fish and chicken. Watch the beef and pork. No fried foods. Lots of vegetables and fruits," he said.

"Not on the cruise. I'm eating everything that doesn't moo or oink. My pipes are clean right now and I'm going to take care of them. I promise. But for that two weeks, I won't be held down to some silly diet," she declared.

"For that two weeks, I won't say a word," the doctor said. "As long as you take your medicine from now on."

Hannah moaned. "I hate pills."

"I hate funerals." He winked at her.

"You win," she smiled. "You all look like a bunch of buzzards hovering around me. Go home. I'll be fine. Just don't forget to come get me the minute they say I can get out of this paradise."

"Nanna, we were worried. You kept talking about babies and granddad," Kim said.

"I was put under once before. Back when I had the twins. That's the way they did things. I kept thinking it was that time and that Jesse was dead. I didn't want him to be dead. And I thought Karen was Mother. Didn't realize how much she's looking like Mother these days. Lord, I'll be glad when they bring supper. Jell-O! Even that sounds good, and I don't like it."

Sue tucked a strand of gray hair behind Hannah's ear. "Nanna, I don't mean to burst your bubble, but I can't go on a cruise right now and neither can Mother. She and Tillman have their heads together over this new business and I'm still helping with the fields, plus the garden is still producing. I just can't go. Can we wait until fall and then things will slow down?"

"You are not invited, so don't get your panties in a kink," Hannah said.

Sue was stunned. "You are going alone?"

"What fun would that be? No, ma'am, I'm not going alone. I'm taking my friends with me. Kim can fix all the arrangements. A senior cruise. I don't want a bunch of kids running around screaming and yelling. That would be worse than men with sagging butts."

John laughed.

Sue blushed.

"Kim, you get it all arranged. Six weeks from the day I get out, or as close to that as the next cruise is ready. Now go home and let an old woman enjoy her Jell-O, and come back to see me tomorrow...after the fruit stand is closed. I don't need buzzards around me." Hannah shooed them out of the room and shut her eyes again, but sleep wouldn't come. She was awake and every gear in her mind was well oiled, ready for action.

CHAPTER SEVENTEEN

"Happy birthday to you," a room full of people sang; off-key, out of tune, rich baritone, perfect soprano, young and old all blended together to sound absolutely lovely in Karen's ears. It had been two weeks since her mother's surgery and Hannah was even bossier and spicier than before. She said what she thought, when she thought it, and everything was a hoot to her. Karen had always loved her mother, but now she adored her. Hannah being alive when Karen turned sixty was the best present of all.

"And now it's time for candles." Luke and Kim worked together to light all sixty on top of a triple-layer chocolate cake with rich chocolate icing.

"Y'all got the fire department on call?" Edith asked.

Karen smiled. "It's not that bad. Wait until *your* birthday. We'll put all eighty on your cake."

"And I'll blow out every one in one breath," Edith declared.

"They're all lit. Make a wish," Kim said.

"I've already got everything. There's nothing to wish for," she said.

"Then wish for a wonderful crop next year," Kim said.

"Just blow them out before they heat up the place more and melt down into my wonderful icing," Sue said.

Karen inhaled deeply and blew until there was no more air in her lungs and smoke filled the room but there wasn't a single candle still burning.

"Never underestimate the power of a strong woman," she said breathlessly.

"Amen," Hannah murmured.

Kim motioned toward the bar. "Momma's choice tonight. Mexican buffet, which comes before cake."

"Not for me. I'm having a slice of that cake right now. It's my birthday and I want dessert first. Momma always let me do that on my birthday when I was a little girl," Karen said.

"Yes, I did, and if you want your cake first tonight, then have at it," Hannah agreed.

"Well, I'm getting into those tacos," Edith said. "Y'all have to try my watermelon salsa. I hadn't made it in years, but it turned out pretty good considering that the watermelon wasn't as good as I like it to be."

"What's in it?" Sue asked.

"Take the juice of one lime and add it to two cups of diced watermelon, one cup of diced and peeled cucumber, three or four sliced green onions, a couple of tablespoons of fresh cilantro that's been cut very fine, two teaspoons of jalapeno peppers cut up just as fine, or more if you want it hotter, and a teaspoon of sugar. It's the best thing in the world with fresh fried corn tortilla chips," Virgie said. "I haven't had that since...mercy...must be twenty years ago."

"At least," Myrtle said. "My momma's been gone thirty years and I think you and Edith made it for her funeral dinner."

"That's right, and we came over here that night and talked about how funny your momma was." Myrtle nodded.

Sue scooped some on her plate and tasted it on the tip of a triangular-shaped chip. She nodded approval and added more, along with a double handful of chips, before moving on down the table to the taco makings. "This is really good. Reckon it would keep if you tried to put it up in jars for the winter?"

"Don't know. It'll keep three days past eternity in the refrigerator. At least that's what they say, but it's never lasted that long for us," Virgie said.

Luke nudged Kim with his elbow. "Let's take ours out on the patio."

"Oh, no, I'm not missing a single story."

"They won't tell anything good with us in the room. Remember, boys aren't allowed," Luke said.

"We'll tell stories, but not the real juicy ones," Virgie laughed. "You can hear all about our watermelon salsa or even our tomato-based salsa."

"What's in the tomato recipe?" Hannah asked.

"Six cans or three quarts of canned tomatoes, two onions the size of a tennis ball, sixteen ounces of jalapeno peppers or one pint if you've canned them yourself, a tablespoon and a half of garlic powder, a teaspoon and a half of both black pepper and salt, and some cilantro chopped fine if you want. Makes a gallon," Sue said. "I found the recipe but it didn't say just how to make it. Just stir it all up?"

Myrtle shook her head. "Oh, no. You put the peppers, juice and all in a blender with the onions and turn it up high until it looks like you've blended a dozen bullfrogs. Pour that into a gallon tea pitcher. Once that hot stuff gets into the plastic, you can't use it for anything else so don't use one you're planning on using for tea later. Then you just barely blend the tomatoes. You want a few chunks left in them so you just hit the button a couple of times. Add that to the pitcher of onions and peppers. Put in the cilantro if you use that stuff. My family don't like it. And then the garlic powder, salt and pepper. Stir it up and put it in jars. Store them in the refrigerator and they'll keep forever or until the kids find them," Myrtle told her.

"We'll make some. This goes really good on the tacos, doesn't it?" Sue piled even more watermelon salsa on top of her food.

"Yes, it does. Reckon they'll have tacos on the cruise?" Virgie asked.

"I don't care if they serve cream of cow poop soup, I'm so excited to be going," Edith said.

"Got your list made for what you're taking to wear to them fancy dinners every night?" Myrtle asked.

"We're going shopping next week, so I'll find something then," Virgie said.

"Something to make those old men's eyes pop right out of their heads, right?" Hannah laughed.

"You got it." Edith raised her glass of lemonade in a toast and all four clicked glasses together.

John led the way to the living room, where he and Sue set their plates on the coffee table and sat cross-legged on the floor.

"So what do you want for your birthday coming up next month?" John asked softly.

"Me? Absolutely nothing. Nanna came through the surgery." She nodded toward the kitchen, where the four elderly women were deep into conversation about their upcoming cruise. "Kim and Luke are happy." She tilted her head toward the patio where Kim had finally decided she and Luke should take their supper. "Edith told me that there's talk in town that the twins belong to him. Wonder who started that?" Sue's eyes twinkled. "And Mother has found her calling in her new venture. Did I tell you that she's going to remodel the garage and put in a special jelly shop this fall so she can sell stuff all winter? What more could a woman want than that on her fortieth birthday?"

"I read in one of those hospital magazines that some women get all depressed when they are forty and look back on their lives," he said.

"I don't think it's going to affect me like that. Twenty did, though. I was pregnant with Kim. We'd had my birthday party at the restaurant in the hotel a few days before the actual day and no one remembered my actual birthday. Then Jeff came home and asked me if I wanted to go for ice cream and I figured his family was going to surprise me with some to-do. But they didn't. It was just plain old ice cream, and Jeff didn't even tell me happy birthday until he noticed the day on the calendar just before he came to bed that night," Sue said.

John kissed her on the cheek. "That would have been a letdown."

"It's no big thing twenty years later." Sue laughed. "Besides, it made the thirtieth much easier. Everyone sent flowers and called. Kim made me a homemade card out of macaroni glued to construction paper, which I still have all packed away."

"When we get done, let's sneak out and go shoot a game of pool," John said.

"Is that kosher? Shouldn't we stay until the last dog is dead, since it's Mother's birthday?" Sue asked.

Karen yelled from the kitchen. "Get on out of here. I'll never know you are gone. And I'm sorry I didn't remember you on the actual day of your twentieth birthday. I'll make it up to you on your fortieth."

"I swear you do have radar." Sue laughed.

"Never doubt it for a minute, and it gets even sharper after you are sixty," Karen told her.

A hot summer breeze kicked up and floated the aroma of his aftershave to her nose as they walked toward his truck. It was woodsy and sexy combined. Much like John: common country boy and sexy to boot.

"So what do you really want for your birthday? I was thinking about an engagement ring."

"Oh, no!" she said.

"Is that a rejection?" he asked.

"It's…I can't…John, please don't ask me that…not now."

"Why? I'm in love with you," he said.

"John, I can't explain. I just can't. I love you, but I couldn't do that to you. You don't understand," she said.

"Then explain it to me," he said tersely.

She leaned against the rear fender of the truck. "I can't. You don't know what happened all those years ago. You can't take a chance like that."

"Then tell me what happened." He drew her close.

"I can't. I've got to go. I'm sorry." She pulled away and stumbled back to the party.

She slipped in the front door and went straight to the bathroom, where she slid down the back of the door and put her head into her hands and wept. The party broke up just after ten o'clock. Kim, Luke, and Karen washed dishes and cleaned up, and then Luke went home. Karen kicked off her sandals and eased down into the corner of the sofa.

"I'm going to take a shower," Hannah said. "Happy birthday again, Karen."

"The best ever," Karen mumbled.

Hannah yelled up the hall when she found the bathroom door locked. "Somebody locked this door. Bring an ice pick so I can flip the trigger."

"I'll be right there," Kim hollered back.

Sue unlocked the door and opened it.

"What happened to you?" Hannah asked.

Kim's eyes widened. "Are you all right, Momma? Where is John?"

"Well, he's sure not in here with me, and besides, it's over," Sue said.

Kim grabbed her in a hug and pulled her out of the bathroom into the hallway, then one step at a time to the living room.

Hannah followed right behind them.

Karen got up from the kitchen table and followed the parade into the living room where they all sat down and waited for Sue to speak. Her eyes were swollen, her makeup smeared, and her face a study in pure misery.

Finally, she opened her mouth. "Momma, would you ever marry again?"

"No, ma'am!" Karen said. "I'd rather be a mistress. They are treated better," Karen said.

"What?" Hannah asked.

"Daniel Tarleton broke me from sucking eggs. I'll never remarry, but someday in the future when they write my obituary they can say that so-and-so was my special friend."

"Bravo for you," Kim said.

"And your mother? If she wants to be a mistress instead of a wife?" Hannah asked.

"I can live with it. I was determined not to like John," Kim said. "I loved my father, and I wouldn't want anyone to take his place. Something about this place clears the mind and makes a person be honest with themselves, doesn't it? But this isn't about us. It's about you, Momma, so what happened? We thought you left with John and then we find you in the bathroom, and you look horrible, by the way."

Sue picked up a tissue from the end table and dabbed at her face. "It all ended tonight. I'm so sorry," she whispered.

"For what?" Hannah asked. "What did John do to upset you this bad?"

"John didn't do a thing and he's a wonderful man."

"Then what is all this about?" Karen asked.

"It's about me, not him. He's perfect. He said he loves me and wanted to know if I want an engagement ring for my birthday."

"And?" Kim held her breath.

"Start from the beginning," Hannah said. "You two were fine when you left here hand in hand. What in the devil happened out there?"

"We made it to his truck and he asked me what I really wanted for my birthday and mentioned an engagement ring. I've only known him a couple of months, but I've fallen in love with him and I can't marry him, because he'll die in a car crash if I do."

"Bull!" Hannah said. "Just because Jeff died in that wreck doesn't mean John would too. Has the heat fried your brain? I told you to wear a hat when you went out."

Kim frowned. "Momma, be sensible. Things don't happen like that. That was a one-time incident. Just because you marry a man doesn't mean he's going to die in an accident like that."

"Yes, it does," Sue said.

"Where do you get such a crazy notion? Like Kim said, it's a one-time thing," Hannah said.

"It's already happened twice, and I'm terrified it will happen again," Sue said.

"Twice?" Karen asked.

"Give me a minute," Sue whispered.

They waited in silence.

"That summer you went to Italy, Mother. It starts then. Remember that boy you said was too wild for me?"

"I remember." Karen nodded.

"Well, you went to Italy. He was eighteen and I was sixteen." Sue paused. "I was supposed to stay with Nanna, but I told her I was staying at the house with Daddy. He thought I was at the hotel with Nanna and brought a woman into the house. I caught them and threatened to blow the whistle on him if he didn't buy me that blue Corvette I'd been pestering you about."

"What happened to it? You didn't have it when I came home and you wouldn't let me buy you a car for your birthday," Karen said.

"Corky and I were seeing each other the whole time you were gone, and this is where it gets complicated. He wanted us to elope. It would be the biggest, meanest thing we could do to you for leaving me with Daddy and going to Italy, and to Daddy for bringing a woman into the house."

"Did you?" Karen stammered.

Sue shook her head. "I was sixteen. I didn't want to be married, but besides, down deep I kind of knew just how much of a bad boy he was. He kept saying that we could blackmail Daddy for more than a car and live like kings…that kind of thing. We fought about it all the time. And then one day we drove into town for junk food and I told him he loved my Corvette more than he loved me. We were really screaming and yelling when we got to the house, and I got out, slammed the door, and he took off like a bat out of Hades. A couple of miles from the house, he missed a curve on the way and hit a telephone pole. Totaled the car. Killed him instantly. Broke his neck. His sister was livid when she saw me at the graveside services. Called me names and said I was responsible for everything. Daddy ranted and raved for two hours about me letting my boyfriend total the car before I was even old enough to legally drive the thing. Daddy told the policeman that he'd lent the car to Corky to run an errand for him and the insurance took care of the rest before you ever got home."

"Good Lord. I knew that boy got killed, but it was never mentioned in the papers about your car." Hannah exhaled loudly.

"Daddy fixed that part really well. No one ever knew," Sue said.

"What happened then?" Kim asked.

Sue inhaled deeply. "I decided that Corky's sister was right. I had been a spoiled rich brat my whole life, so I changed my whole lifestyle. I studied hard. Got a scholarship. Paid my own way and didn't take money from you all. Met Jeff and married him. Then he died in that horrible drunk-driver accident. Two of them. I can't take another chance."

"Bull!" Hannah said bluntly. "That boy's death had nothing to do with Jeff's, and Jeff's will have no bearing on John's. If you want to use that excuse and wallow around in a pity pool, that's your business. But don't try to sell it to me. We all made mistakes when we were young. Karen had an affair. Kim is pregnant. I was in the same boat when I got pregnant with the twins. You had a couple of bumps in your road of life. So have we all, but they were bumps, not stop signs. They slow us down, make us think a bit about our mistakes. They don't keep us from moving forward."

"Nanna!" Sue exclaimed.

"Well, if you're lookin' for sympathy from me, you're out of luck. I say, get back up on your feet and stop this caterwaulin'. Kim faced her problem better than you're doing, and you are nigh onto forty. John might die in a car crash, but it's not to punish you for your sins. He might live to be a hundred and get hanged for robbing a bank. You don't control those things, girl. That's God's job. Let Him do it, and you climb on out of that pity pot before you drown."

"I thought you'd understand," Sue said.

"Don't you take that tone with me." Hannah shook her finger under Sue's nose.

"I agree with Nanna," Kim said. "That was hard luck, having your boyfriend die like that. And then the same thing, in a way, happening with Dad. But that's in the past. You going to let all that destroy a future of happiness?"

"What about you? You going to tell Marshall Neville he's the father of your babies? You going to marry Luke?" Sue snapped.

Karen threw up a palm toward Sue. "This isn't about Kim tonight. It's about you, so don't be turning the tables. Decide what you want and go fight for it."

"Luke and I have talked about Marshall. It's only right that he know about the babies. I plan to call. I don't want child support, and I don't want to give them his name, but I do think he should know. Luke and I are taking the rest a day at a time and you'll be the first to know when we make a decision," Kim admitted.

"So now it's all out in the open. All of our hidden secrets," Sue said.

"Unless someone else has something to say," Hannah said.

Sue wiped away the last remnants of tears. "I've got somewhere to go. Thanks. All of you. Don't wait up for me. It might be a long night."

"I don't think it'll take that long to convince John that you changed your mind," Kim said.

"It might, but he's worth the battle if I can have the prize when the fight is finished," Sue threw over her shoulder as she headed for the door.

The lights were out when she knocked on the front door. Mosquitoes the size of vultures buzzed around her ears. She swatted at them while she waited. Finally, she heard John swear as he fumbled down the hall in the darkness.

He rubbed at his eyes and stared at her. "Sue?"

He wore a pair of thin cotton pajama bottoms, but his broad, muscular chest was bare. He ran his fingers through his bedroom hair and asked, "Is something wrong? Hannah? Is she all right?"

"Everyone is fine. We need to talk. Would you come out here on the porch with me?" she asked.

"And get eat up by bugs? No thank you, but you can come inside. I'll make a pot of coffee."

She opened the screen door and followed him to the kitchen, where he turned on a light and set about making coffee. In moments, the smell filled the kitchen and her stomach growled.

He poured two cups and sat down at the kitchen table, motioning for her to join him. "Do you talk first or do I?"

"What could you have to say?" Sue asked.

"I understand why you took off like a scalded hound tonight." He sipped the coffee. "I'm just a hardworking country boy. I've amassed a little fortune, by my standards, that is. By yours, it's just a lima bean compared to a fifty-pound watermelon. I'm a rancher. That's what I am and I can't change any of it. Now, you can tell me all those things in your words and we'll shake hands and be friends."

She set the coffee cup down with a thud.

"Bull!" She sounded just like Hannah. "I came here to tell you why I was confounded, confused, and scared to death of another commitment and you sure don't know me very well if you think I'm materialistic."

The story that tumbled out was much easier to tell the second time. When she finished, he was grinning from ear to ear.

He reached across the table and covered her hands with his. "And I thought I was the problem. Honey, Hannah was right. We don't have that kind of control. The fact that a wild-natured little sixteen-year-old girl was out to show her father how much devilment she could get into to punish him or the fact that the same girl lost her husband in a similar wreck doesn't mean that's my portion if you marry me."

"So you still interested in buying me that ring?" she asked.

"I am." He looked deep into her blue eyes.

"What if I want to be engaged for a long time? Like a year?"

"Then we'll wait a year," he said. "I love you, Sue. I think Miz Norma knew what she was doing when she fixed things so you all would come out here. She wanted the two of us to get together."

"Really?" Sue asked.

"I do. Come here, darlin'. We'll talk about rings and weddings later. Right now I just want to hold you," John said.

She walked around the table and curled up in his lap. "Right now, I just want to feel your arms around me."

He tipped her face back and kissed her. "I'll always be a rancher and farmer."

"I'll always be rich whether I like it or not, but I'm going to be a good farmer as well, and I don't want to rush."

"Are we talking about the rest of tonight or our lives?" he asked.

"Both," she whispered.

CHAPTER EIGHTEEN

The girls were all out of the house, and Hannah was alone for the first time all summer and she didn't like it.

Kim's bedroom door was open, so she went inside and sat on the bed. Everything was neat: the bed made, no clothing tossed on the floor, the dresser and chest of drawers dusted, with items on the top arranged in perfect alignment. Kim was at the church. Bible school would start that night and she was helping put the last-minute details together. Something about decorating T-shirts and getting the kids' names written on the back. Luke was at the school, getting his room ready for the new school year, which would start in two weeks. She left Kim's room and crossed the hall into what was now hers but had been Norma's. She opened the closet doors and stared at the shoe boxes full of letters.

"I miss my friend," she said aloud. "That's it! I miss you, Norma. I miss writing all those letters. It was wonderful to put on paper what was going on around me, and now you are gone and I can't write and tell you the most important news we've ever had," she kept talking. "I need a place to talk to you when good things or even bad ones happen. I've always shared everything with you, and I miss it. You don't even have a tombstone in a graveyard where I can come and visit with you. Heaven don't have a phone line or an address where I can send a letter."

She looked out the glass wall in the living room. "A memorial! That's it! John said the first day we got here that I'd know when the time was right to scatter your ashes and I've thought and thought about it and nothing came to mind. But if I had a memorial right out there in the backyard, I could scatter them and I'd have a place where your spirit is to talk to you."

Grabbing up the phone book, she looked up landscaping specialists. She found a starting place and dialed the phone number. A young woman answered all her questions and asked several of her own. When she understood that Hannah wanted a memory garden she said she was actually just returning from Coleman and was in Milburn. She could bring her books by and visit with Hannah in the next hour, if that would be convenient.

"Yes, it would," Hannah said and hung up.

"It's an omen, Norma. I figured it all out and the woman can come right now so it was meant to be." She hummed as she made a pitcher of fresh lemonade and cleared off the table so she could look at pictures of memory gardens.

She slung the door open before the lady had time to knock and motioned her inside. "Come right in. You'll be Gloria, right? Well, I want flowers for all seasons. And lights too, and come on back through the living room and look out the back windows. That's what we've got to work with, and I want a fence," she said, breathlessly.

"I can see you pretty well know what you want," Gloria said.

"Oh, yes, I do. Just put your books on the table and have a seat. Lemonade?"

"That sounds wonderful." Gloria unloaded her books and pulled out a chair. "Tell me about the person this garden is going to honor."

"Norma was my best friend and I miss her, so I want a place where I can go talk to her. She's been cremated because she hated the idea of being buried, so her ashes will be scattered all over this garden when it's finished. We wrote to each other faithfully for the past sixty years and talked on the phone once a week. I miss her, and it sounds crazy, but I want a place where I can go sit and visit with her anytime I want."

Gloria nodded. "That's what a memory garden is for. To remember the loved one and feel their presence when you go there. How big do you want this garden to be?"

"Big enough for several people to sit inside the fence. I'm thinking three benches arranged in a seating area at the front beside the big stone with room at the back for flowers and all. Maybe include the patio inside it and extend it on out toward the trees."

"White fence?"

"I think verdigris would be better. Can you get that?"

"I can. Let it blend with the trees and the house and not stand out like a sore thumb. So how tall?"

"This big." Hannah held her hand up.

"Three feet. How about a soft-pink granite stone? Maybe a table with those three benches where you can put your lemonade while you visit," Gloria said.

"I like that." Hannah smiled. "I can retain you to take care of the flower planting each season, can't I? Norma loved her flowers."

"I would be glad to do that." Gloria nodded. "We'll need a sprinkler system."

"There's one in the front yard already."

"Will the well system support all this?" Gloria asked.

"They tell me there are three wells on the place, but if that isn't enough, then I'll drill another one," Hannah said. "Now, let's look at those books. I want to see pretty pictures. When can it all be finished?"

"Six weeks, max. That's if I have to bring in a well man. Five if what you've got will take care of the water. You can choose a monument today from the books and decide what you want engraved on it. That usually takes three to five weeks."

"I'm leaving on a cruise in three weeks. Maybe it will be done by the time I return. Then I can tell Norma all about my trip," Hannah said.

"Yes, ma'am." Gloria opened her books.

❖ ❖ ❖

Kim and three other young women worked in the church kitchen, painting names on the backs of T-shirts for Vacation Bible School. Her main job would be playing the piano for the songs they'd sing every evening, but she would probably be called upon to help with the crafts when she wasn't playing. They sat around a six-foot table, T-shirts spread out in front of them.

"So when are you going to marry Luke?" Betsy asked. She was a tall, leggy blonde with brown eyes and freckles across her nose.

"Who says I'm going to marry him?" Kim countered.

"That was a rude question, anyway, and none of our business, but when are you going to marry him?" Leah asked. She had long, black hair and twinkling brown eyes. She was barely five feet tall and had delicate, almost child-like features.

"Mind your manners. Kim won't play the piano for us if we make her mad, and God knows we can't play. Which brings me to the question, when are you going to marry Luke?" Darah pushed a strand of red hair back behind her ear and giggled.

Kim shook her head. "I really don't know."

"Hmmmph, I know what you mean. When the preacher said that about obeying and until death parting us, I almost ran out the door. Sometimes I wish I had when my kids get to bickering," Darah said.

"You've got kids?" Kim asked.

"Two of them. Four and six years old."

"But you're only twenty," Kim protested.

"Thank you, darlin', but I'm twenty-six. Had Jennifer when I was nineteen. Quinton and I've had our share of fights, let me tell you, but all in all, it's working out pretty good. He adores the kids and most of the time I love him. Today is the exception. Today he is a stubborn mule," Darah told her.

"Don't tell us. He's going fishing every night this week so he doesn't have to help with Bible school," Leah said.

"You got it, honey. I hope all he catches is a massive dose of poison ivy and chigger bites," Darah answered.

"Whew, you know how to put a curse on a man, don't you?" Kim said.

"Yes, ma'am, she does." Betsy picked up another shirt.

"Have you both got kids too?" Kim asked.

"I've got one. Granger is six. Gage is my husband and he teaches at Milburn junior high with Luke. We tried for years to have a child and it looks like Granger is the only one we're going to get, since the procedure costs so much money," Betsy said.

"Lord, that kid could scale a glass wall on a rainy day. Don't know why you'd want more," Darah said.

"And both of yours would be leading him up that wall." Betsy laughed.

"They're the devils that need Bible school. My Laynie is a saint," Leah said.

"Laynie is a little blonde-haired saint now. Wait until she grows up and falls in love with Granger. He'll teach her the ways of the world," Betsy told her.

Leah pointed a paintbrush across the table. "You better keep that future hoodlum away from my daughter."

"So you're having twins?" Darah asked Kim.

"That's what the doctor says. My great-grandmother had twins the first time, but they both died right after birth. That was more than sixty years ago and medicine wasn't what it is today," Kim said.

"You want boys or girls or one of each?" Leah asked.

"They'll be the same. Identical, the doctor says. So it's either two girls or two boys."

"Drop down on your knees and pray right now in this church basement that it's girls and they're like Laynie and not Granger," Leah said.

Kim smiled. "I don't care if they're ornery boys. If this set isn't, I hope I can have another set that is. All I've ever been around is girls, but I can learn what to do with boys. My great-grandmother is an only child. My grandmother is an only child and so is my mother, and I don't have brothers or sisters. I want a house full of kids."

"Spoken like a woman with no kids," Darah said. "Tell us that story when Luke is off fishing every night during Bible school and you've got two sets of twins trying to swing from the rafters."

Luke poked his head into the room. "Hey, can I steal the music director for lunch?"

"Sure, we're about to close up shop here anyway. We've all got things to do this afternoon, but only if you'll tell us when the wedding date is," Leah teased.

Luke blushed, his dark skin deepening into a maroon. "That is totally up to Kim."

"So?" Luke asked as they drove west toward Tishomingo.

"So what?"

"So when is the wedding? I'm crazy about you and all you have to do is name the time and date. I'll be there, whether it's eloping to Cancun over a weekend or a full-blown affair at the church."

"I'm pregnant," she reminded him.

"Did you tell those women the baby isn't mine?"

"Babies. Twins. And no, I didn't tell them. I'm flustered about the way everyone thinks they belong to you. How could they? Even if they were, we would have had to sleep together the first night I got into town. What does that make me?"

"Pregnant," he grinned as he pulled into a parking spot at the Sonic in Tishomingo, rolled down the window, and pushed a button.

"Welcome to Sonic. I'll take your order when you are ready," a tinny voice said.

Luke looked over at Kim.

"Two hot dogs with no onions, fries, and a cherry lime-ade," she said.

"You hear that?" Luke asked the speaker.

"Yes, sir. Anything else?"

"A double bacon cheeseburger with fries and the biggest Coke you have."

"Be right out," the voice said.

"So?" Luke slipped his hand over hers. "Cancun or the church?"

"What if you don't like me after? What if you don't want to be a father and a husband both?"

"I might not like you, but I'll always love you, and when I don't like you we'll figure it all out on a daily basis and fix it."

"I had good parents. Momma and Daddy were good together, but I had sorry grandparents. My granddad, Daniel, was a womanizer and my grandmother ignored it. I'm not like that. I'd scalp you if you ever cheated on me."

"I love you, Kim. I will never cheat on you. And I mean that with all my heart and soul," he whispered.

"I don't want to mess it up, and with my granddad's genes, I could. I might be the one cheating on you."

"No, you won't. And if we mess it up, we'll fix it," he said seriously. "I want to marry you before school starts in two weeks. That way I can go through the rest of this pregnancy with you. We'd be married six months when the babies are born. But I'm not going to mention it again. When you get it all settled in your mind, you tell me what you want."

"You're willing for that?"

"I am."

"Thank you," she said.

"Now, tell me, have you met Granger yet?"

"No, but I've been forewarned. They say he's a case on wheels."

"Honey, he's a hellion, but he's got a voice like an angel. Wait until you hear him sing. Sounds like it's coming right out of heaven. If he's not the next big Nashville star I'll eat my work boots."

"And Laynie? Can she sing?"

"Looks like an angel. Acts like one. All prissy and golden-haired. Couldn't carry a tune in a galvanized milk bucket," Luke said.

Kim thought about the day she'd been wishing for a sign and Hannah had called to say she was going to Oklahoma to a farm. Could it have really only been two months ago? She felt as if she had come home to stay.

The carhop brought their food to the car and they ate in comfortable silence. Afterward, Luke drove back to Milburn, where her mother's van was parked. But he didn't hop right out and rush around the truck to open the door for her. Instead, he left the engine running and turned to face her.

"I don't know how to say it. Didn't want to back there because there were folks all around us and it's very private."

"Are you dying?" she whispered softly.

He chuckled. "No, I'm not dying, but the summer I was fifteen, I got the mumps."

She slapped him on the arm. "You scared me like that just to tell me you had the mumps. Luke, don't ever, ever do that again. What's the big deal with mumps? I got the chicken pox when I was thirteen. Momma said she had to drape the mirrors to preserve my vanity and her sanity. I moaned and groaned and carried on like a movie star with a zit and no makeup artist. So your big news is you got the mumps?"

"Yes, that's it." Luke sighed.

"I can still love you even after that."

"Kim, I really did get the mumps. Big-time, and they went down on me. Do you know what that means to a teenage boy?"

"No, but I know what chicken pox meant to a teenage girl."

"It meant that the fever caused me to be sterile. Well, almost, anyway. There's maybe one chance in two million that I could ever father a child. The doctor says it's not impossible, but it would take a small miracle for me to ever be a father."

"Who knows?" she finally whispered.

"John knows, but he's the only one other than my grandpa. It was in the summer, and no one ever knew the extent of what happened. I never told anyone."

"Is that why you let everyone think you are the father? Is that why you want to marry me?"

"I would want to marry you no matter what. I love you, Kim. I really do, and I want to spend my life with you. I just wanted you to understand, there probably will never be any more children."

"I've always thought I wanted a house full of kids," she said.

"We can buy all the babies you want. Adoption is expensive, but we'll afford a houseful if that's what you want," he said.

"Or maybe that miracle will occur sometime down the road," she said.

"It could, but don't count on it."

"Is the offer still good that I can think about all this and tell you when I'm ready?"

"As long as I've got breath in my body." He leaned across the space and kissed her.

❖ ❖ ❖

At the supper table that night, Hannah refilled her salad bowl instead of reaching for a second piece of fried chicken. "I hate this old low-fat dressing. Can't you figure out a way to make something that tastes good and won't kill me?"

"You know the rule, Nanna," Sue answered. "If it tastes good, throw it out. If it tastes like crap, eat it."

"Amen. So what did you get accomplished today?"

"The fall crop is in the ground. We're under a burn ban. No rain for more than a month now and everything is tinder dry. Kind of scary. They've already had a couple of massive grass fires over around Nida. No houses were burned, though."

"And you, Kim? Got the little kiddos ready for Bible school tonight?"

"Everything is ready there, but I've got a problem. Please promise you won't mention it in front of Luke."

"Want us to prick our fingers and sign an affidavit in blood?" Hannah asked.

"That might not be a bad idea," Kim said seriously.

Hannah laid her fork down. "What is it?"

"He wants to marry me," Kim said.

"And that's a big private secret? Honey, everyone knows that. Just seeing you together is evidence that you belong together. Plus, most folks think those babies are his, and by the way, you need to buy some maternity clothes. Don't be forcing those babies to live in cramped quarters."

"No, that's not the secret. He swears he loves me and wants to marry me anyway, but I'm scared that it's just *because* I'm pregnant. He told me today he had mumps when he was a teenager. I didn't know they could do this 'go down' stuff and make a man sterile but it happened. There's one chance in a million he could ever father a child, so is he really in love with me, or am I just providing a wife and fatherhood both? He says not. Are you going to say 'Bull!,' Nanna?"

Hannah said, "Yep, that's what I'm going to say. Listen to your heart. It doesn't have ears or eyes. Just feelings, and most of the time they are very true. Luke adores you. Wake up and smell the bacon frying, girl. You don't get the guarantee of tomorrow. Today is all you have. Don't waste it worrying. Enjoy it. Don't go stumbling up to the Pearly Gates in your spotless martyr robes. Go sliding up there in a worn-out, used-up body, screaming to the top of your lungs, 'Hallelujah, I made it and I've used everything I had while I was on earth, so open the doors and let me in!' That's the way to live."

"But, Nanna." Kim finally got a word in edgewise. "I wanted a house full of kids."

"But, Kim." Hannah narrowed her eyes. "What you want and what you get are often two different things. If you want a houseful then go adopt an orphanage or else go to bed with Luke a million times and hope it's twins again when you reach the magic number."

Karen snorted and then giggled. It turned into a full-fledged contagious laugh that had them all roaring.

"How did we ever live anywhere else?" Kim finally wiped at her eyes.

"We didn't. We survived. It wasn't until we came to Emet that we began to live. And I for one am not going back to anything less. Thank you, Norma! Now let me tell you all about my day and the memory garden that is going in right beside the patio," Hannah said.

CHAPTER NINETEEN

It looked like the devil's tongue licking its way across the rolling hills, red with yellow tinges, lapping out, devouring every bit of grass, trees, still hungry and dancing to a steady, fast pace as if the music it heard was a fast Irish reel. They'd known for an hour it was on the way, and John and Luke, both members of the volunteer fire department, had been out there fighting it all day. The latest news had been a thirty-second call from John, telling them to go to Tishomingo and stay there until he let them know it was safe to come back home. Just get out of Emet, because the fire was eating up the twelve-mile prairie and the south wind was bringing it straight to them.

"I'm not seeing these homes burn to the ground if there's a thing we can do. We're four able-bodied women who can do something about it. We can always run if it gets too hot," Hannah said.

"Nanna, Norma must have seen fires and she had to have written to you about them. What do we do?" Kim asked.

"Wet down some bandannas to put over our noses, like the old bandits did in the movies. That'll keep us from inhaling some of the smoke. Sue, is the plow still attached to the tractor?"

"Yes, it is." Sue nodded.

"Then you get on that tractor, go through the fence out by the orchard separating our place from Luke's, and drive over to the south side of his property. There's a barbed-wire fence between him and the next ranch. I want you to drop that plow and tear up the earth right next to the fence. Is the boom sprayer full for irrigatin' tomorrow, Karen?"

She nodded. "Hitched to Norma's truck."

"You take it right behind Sue's firebreak and spray down the grass as far as the boom will work. That way, if the fire keeps coming it'll hit dirt and then water and hopefully it'll die right there," Hannah said.

Sue and Karen grabbed bandannas from the stack on the cabinet, wet them down, and hurried outside.

"What about me?" Kim asked.

"You and I are going to wet down our property line to the south in case that devil gets through the firebreak and comes right at us. We'll hook up every sprinkler and hose we've got and water down our fence line," Hannah said. "But if that smoke gets to be too much, you will come in the house. We can't endanger those babies."

Sue fired up the tractor, drove through the big gates separating Luke's place from theirs, and was headed toward the section line to the south when she remembered the gates. She left the tractor running and ran back to shut them. The smoke was as heavy as fog, with a south wind whipping it over the land. She was glad the tractor had an air-conditioned cab, just so it would keep the smoke away from her nose, because she was already coughing. She dropped the plow next to the fence line and began to make a firebreak.

She could hear the sirens of fire engines as they whizzed past on the road in front of the fruit stand, sirens blaring as they disappeared into a wall of gray smoke. She hoped this trick would work and they didn't lose the fruit stand and the house. Not when they'd made so many memories in both.

Her cell phone rang and she pulled it out of her pocket. "Hello."

"Are you all away and safe?" John asked.

"You just fight your fires and don't worry about us," she said.

"Sue?"

"We aren't leaving, John. Hannah says we're staying. You got a fight. Take it up with her," Sue told him.

"I'll take it up with you when I get home. What are you doing right now?"

"Plowing a firebreak against Luke's south fence," she answered.

"Dang it, Sue! The fire is coming straight at you. Get off that tractor and get out of there," John yelled.

"Losing connection. Must be the smoke." She hit a button to end the call.

She dialed her mother's cell phone number and Karen answered before it rang a second time. "I can see you. There's smoke between us, but I can see you. Do you think there's enough water in this thing to get us to the end?"

"I hope so. John just called. We're going to have a couple of angry menfolk tonight."

Karen laughed nervously. "I'd rather face two angry men than one ticked-off mother."

"Amen. Speak of the devil. Kim is buzzing in. I'd better take it," Sue said.

"Momma, Luke called and he's really upset." Kim talked before Sue could even say a word.

"I know, but which one is meaner: those two fellers or your nanna?"

Kim giggled. "No contest to that, is there? I'll see you when you get home. The wind is dying down a little, so maybe that will help."

Sue finished plowing and Karen used up all the water in the boom sprayer. They drove back to the yard and parked both vehicles. The wind had begun to subside and the flames were moving slower.

"I'll take that hose. You get in the house and take a shower. If the wind picks up again and it jumps Luke's fence, we'll have to move his cattle over into the orchard."

"Oh, no! If they eat the apples, Nanna will shoot them all," Kim said.

Sue took the hose from her hand. "Go take a shower and get that soot and smoke off you. It can't be good for the babies."

Karen grabbed the hose from Hannah and motioned for her to get in the house. "You won't go on your cruise if you die from smoke inhalation."

Hannah and Kim reached the porch at the same time.

"We whipped it. I know we did," Hannah said.

"What do we do now?" Kim coughed.

"After showers, we'll start supper. I can peel potatoes and you can make the salad. John and Luke are going to be hungry."

Kim shucked out of her clothing right there in the middle of the kitchen floor. She wore white cotton underpants and a white bra, both of which were soaked in sweat.

"Why would they be so angry at us?" she asked.

"Because we didn't obey orders to leave. Even if women have fought for the right to be equals, men will always think they have to protect us. They think we're fragile and can't drive a tractor or a sprayer. Only big, brave men can do that. But mostly they like to be big he-men and they want to be obeyed," Hannah answered.

Sue and Karen had turned off the water and they were on their way to the house when the sound of a truck engine roared into the yard. Dust and smoke mingled as the truck came to a skidding stop.

"What is going on?" John stopped the truck.

"We just turned off the water. Has it died?" Sue asked.

"I told you to leave. I told you to go where it was safe," he yelled.

"Kim?" Luke's eyes searched through the fog-like smoke for her.

"She's at the house. Sucked up some smoke while she manned the water hoses, but she's fine," Sue said without taking her eyes from John's.

"My God, what if we'd lost you?" Luke said.

"That's your fight with Kim. Go to it and have fun. Just get out of my fight with John," Sue told him.

"Why didn't you listen? I'd give up every cow in that pasture and everything I own to keep you safe, and you're out here risking your life for what? A bunch of cows? A blade of grass?" John raised his voice another octave.

"It's mine and I fight for what's mine," she said.

He motioned toward his truck. "Let's get out of this smoke."

She was glad to crawl up in the passenger's seat, shut the door, and inhale air-conditioning, even if it did have the faint odor of burning grass. But if he thought the argument was finished then he'd best think again, because the day had not dawned when he was going to tell her what she could and could not do. Oklahoma had awakened a whole new woman inside Sue DeHaven. One with sass and brass, who'd stand up to a fire bigger than Hades to protect what was hers.

Sue looked him over carefully. "You look like the devil and you need a shower."

His nostrils still flared. His full mouth was a firm pencil line. "So do you."

"I will not obey you, John. I'll work with you, but you're not going to yell 'frog' and expect me to jump. And I want an engagement ring for my birthday," she said.

"What has that got to do with you being reckless and endangering the lives of four women?"

"You said to tell you what and when I wanted. I'm telling you. While I was out there on that tractor, I figured it out. I love you and I want to be married to you. I want an engagement ring for my fortieth birthday and I want to marry you sometime this winter."

He scooted across the seat and wrapped his arms around her. "I love you, Sue. Can't you see that if I'd lost you to this fire, I would have died too?"

"Do I get my engagement ring?"

"Yes, you get your ring. I'm going to take you to the house and then I'm going home to take a shower and cool off before I say anything else, but next time…"

"Next time, darlin', I will do the same thing I did today. Try to save what is ours. I won't give up one inch of what's ours, not if it's in my power to keep it."

"You are some piece of work!" He started the pickup.

"And don't you forget it!"

Luke met Kim coming down the hallway, toweling her long hair dry. She wore a pair of baggy shorts and an oversized T-shirt and smelled like heaven. He looked like he'd been rolled in ashes, stayed too long in the tanning bed, and come up the loser in a dirt clod fight, and smelled like he'd done three rounds of wrestling with the devil.

"Are you all right?" he asked tersely.

"I'm fine. We did it, Luke. We kept it from burning the houses and John's pasture. Nanna and Grandmother moved the cows and I watered everything in sight. Oh, I forgot, the hoses are still out there running. We might be flooding the area," she said excitedly.

"I don't care what you saved, woman. I told you to go away so you'd be safe. Don't you listen to a thing? This relationship isn't going to work if you can't listen."

Kim popped both hands on her hips. "This relationship isn't going to work if you expect me to let my home burn down around my ears when I can prevent it. Nanna is eighty years old, honey, and she was out there working with us. Grandmother is sixty and Momma will be forty in two days. You think I'm going to turn tail and leave them here just because you expect me to listen? If you do, you've got rocks for brains. This is my home, and your house is going to be mine and yours…"

He crossed his arms over his chest. "But it was your life."

"And I'm alive," she said. "Just don't you go thinking you are God, because you sure ain't. What you're going to do is get a shower and then come back over here for supper. Nanna is already peeling potatoes, and I'm about to make a big salad to go with the pot roast and noodles that Momma has started."

"Oh, no, you're not going to get off the hook that easy. You should have left like I told you," he said.

"You want to marry me?" she asked.

"Of course, but that has nothing to do with this."

"Yes, it does. We are a team. We'll work as one. Love as one. Live as one. You'll have to live with the fact that I'm not a hothouse orchid. I'm a plain old marigold and I can stand the heat, even if it's flying out of your sexy eyes." She smiled.

He melted.

"I'm going home and get cleaned up, but this isn't over."

She took two steps forward, wrapped her arms around his neck, and pulled his dirty face down for a long, passionate kiss. "Now it is."

CHAPTER TWENTY

Four ladies sat in lounge chairs on the deck of the cruise ship. Edith and Hannah wore khaki capri pants with yellow shirts and new Nikes on their feet. Virgie declared she was going for style and wanted something to complement her black hair. She wore red walking shorts with a nautical shirt and high heels. Myrtle said style be damned, she'd be comfortable, and opted for an outfit she'd ordered from QVC. It had flowing pajama-cut pants and a long matching tunic of orange and yellow swirls.

"So tell me again what all we're doing. I still can't believe I shopped in New York City." Virgie sighed.

"Seven days of pure luxury," Edith said. "This evening we dine in the fancy place and get to wear our evening gowns. You reckon that fellow over there that's been ogling Virgie ever since we sat down out here will be there in a tux?"

Virgie sat up straighter and picked at imaginary lint on her red shorts. "I told you these distinguished-looking men would like red shorts," she said, the twinkle in her eyes brighter than it had been in months.

"And then tomorrow we'll spend the whole day at sea," Edith continued.

"Or flirting with that 'distinguished-looking man,'" Myrtle teased.

"Sounds like a good way to spend a day to me." Virgie smiled and glanced toward the gray-haired gentleman, who raised a glass of wine at her.

"Then the next day we'll be in St. George's," Edith told her. "Pay attention, Virgie. You might never get another cruise."

Virgie fluffed up her big hair. "Oh, you're just jealous. I told you to go for cheap style rather than expensive taste."

"Never mind her, I'm listening," Myrtle said.

"Then the next day we go to Hamilton and then King's Wharf, and then we spend a day at sea and get back to New York the next morning," Edith said.

"And from there I've got a little surprise," Hannah said. "We're flying to Baltimore and then into Morgantown. I got news that I need to sign papers. So we're going to stay in the Brewer Hotel two nights before we go home. Will that be a problem for anyone?"

"Problem?" Edith shook her head. "It sounds wonderful."

"I've also got a car ready with a driver to take us for sight-seeing. Thought you might like to see the glassware that's been made there for decades and the wineries."

"Can we help you next year with the harvest?" Myrtle laughed.

"Honey, this is a yearly jaunt. Next year let's go on a different cruise. Want to go around the world in forty days?" Hannah asked.

"I could do that in one night with that good-looking man," Virgie said.

"Virgie!" Edith exclaimed.

"Well, I could, and he's winked twice, so I'm going over there to see just who he is."

"I can't believe she's doing that," Edith said.

"What happens on a cruise, stays on a cruise," Hannah told her.

"I think that was the Las Vegas slogan," Myrtle said.

"Could be, but I'm not putting it in the Tishomingo newspaper that Virgie had a hot and heavy fling with a man with a saggin' butt," Hannah said.

"Darlin', at eighty, all men's butts sag." Edith giggled.

Virgie joined them for dinner, declaring the man was an egotistical slob who talked nonstop about his job in New York and never one time tossed a scrap of a compliment her way, much less asked where she was from or what she'd done in her lifetime.

"He's just here to pick up a rich wife." Virgie pouted.

"He might find one. His hair is pretty and he has his own teeth," Virgie said.

"See, he's after a rich wife," Myrtle said.

"How do you know?"

"He's right over there with his arm around a younger woman. Why, she shouldn't even be on this cruise. I bet she's not a day over fifty," Myrtle said.

"Plastic does wonders," Hannah said as she ordered salmon and a baked potato with butter and sour cream. The doctor said she could have all she wanted on the cruise. When she got home, she'd use fake butter and nonfat sour cream. But she'd never get used to it.

"Would you ever have plastic surgery?" Edith asked.

"Mercy, no! I wasn't even going to keep living until I met you ladies and moved all the girls in with me. Emet has been good for us all," Hannah said.

"You were just coming home, that's all," Edith said.

"Guess so. Put down some roots all those years ago and Norma kept them watered," Hannah said.

"Here comes a man with a purpose in his eye," Edith said.

"I am Buford Talley. Could I have the honor of a dance with you?" He stopped and stared down into Hannah's uplifted face.

"That would be very nice," Hannah said.

"He doesn't fill out the backside of his pants," Virgie whispered.

"Long as there's enough there to keep his balance on the dance floor," Hannah said softly.

Buford danced with all four ladies before moving on to the next table. He was smooth and let his partner do the talking. He was there to find a wife who liked to dance and who had money. Hannah was beautiful with her upswept silver hair, but she came from a small town in Oklahoma and worked a watermelon farm. Buford was looking for someone near New York City. Edith was funny, but she too was a retired farmer. Virgie, now that was a wildcat he would have gladly spent the night with, but alas, Buford had only seven nights and he had to find a serious relationship. No nights to waste. Myrtle was so much like his fourth wife, he almost forgot his mission and asked for a moonlight stroll on the deck, but at the last moment changed his mind.

"What was that all about?" Virgie asked.

"He likes to dance and wants a fresh hen every time," Hannah said.

"He's got a lean and hungry look. Betcha he's looking for someone to rob," Virgie said.

"Or marry, which is worse. I heard senior citizens use these cruises to find mates. How'd you like to stir up his Metamucil every night?" Hannah asked.

That set them off into giggles.

By the time they'd eaten breakfast the next morning the ship had docked in Bermuda at St. George. The ladies walked off the ship's steps straight onto Front Street where so many shops and restaurants were located it was hard to decide where to go first. They bought T-shirts with dolphins on them, hats, and costume jewelry. They purchased items for their children and grandchildren and had lunch at an expensive little café specializing in seafood.

That evening they dined on the ship, watching Buford go through another evening of women before finally settling on one who was ninety if she was a day. She was decked out in Armani with diamonds dripping from every finger and earlobe, and even a small tiara set in her Clairol-blonde curls. He nodded at Myrtle but escorted Ms. Richie-Rich out of the dining room when the music stopped.

"Guess he'll be stirring up his own Metamucil. I don't see her doing much for him," Myrtle said.

"Maybe she will have dementia bad enough not to request a prenup," Virgie said. "God, my feet are tired. I'm going to my room, sit in that Jacuzzi for an hour, and then fall asleep."

"Honey, if you stay in that Jacuzzi more than ten minutes, you'll fall asleep and drown," Hannah said.

That woman Buford had singled out looked so familiar. Hannah could hardly keep her eyes off the lady. She was almost asleep that evening when it came to her in the darkness of the stateroom just whom Buford was keeping company with. If it hadn't been so late she would have knocked on all three doors and shared the news with the ladies.

The next day they visited Hamilton, the capital of Bermuda. At midday Hannah hailed a taxi to take them to the Pink

Beach Club for lunch and an afternoon of walking on the white sands in their bare feet. On the third day, they visited King's Wharf. Edith bought an Irish woolen sweater, swearing the whole time it was much too expensive but that it would serve as her winter coat, no colder than it got in southern Oklahoma. Virgie bought two nice pieces of jewelry. Diamond earrings and a matching pendant. Edith opted for clothing and Hannah found matching hats for her and the girls.

They met in the formal dining room again, and Buford was there with his new lady friend, who kept him on a short leash. Again he winked at Myrtle but made no attempt to talk to her.

"So tomorrow we are at sea, and we'll wake up in New York the next morning," Virgie said. "I don't know when I've ever had so much fun in my whole life."

"I'm homesick," Hannah said. "I'm ready to be back in Emet. Can't wait to tell the girls about the trip, and how much fun we've had, but I'm ready to go home."

"You're not homesick for Morgantown?" Edith asked.

"Not in the least."

Edith sighed. "That was the biggest part of your life, girl, and you don't miss it? I've loved this trip. It's been wonderful, but I'm homesick too. I just plain miss Emet."

"Me too," Hannah said.

"Here we are sitting in the lap of luxury and missing sorting squash. Doesn't make a lot of sense, does it?" Myrtle said.

"The lap of luxury is nice. It makes a real good substitute for happiness. We'll be ready to go again by the time we bring in next year's crop, but a lifetime of luxury doesn't bring happiness. It just brings fun. The two are very different," Hannah said.

"I don't think I want a round-the-world cruise though. Let's just do the weeklong thing," Virgie said.

"I'd come back here every single year. Be nice to see if Buford outlives his sugar momma," Myrtle whispered behind her hand.

"Oh, they won't be on another cruise. She'll keep him hopping like a little froggy until he dies of a heart attack," Hannah said. "After that she'll put on all that paste and Armani that she got on sale at the Goodwill store and find her another one. She's not as rich as she looks, ladies. They may wind up living in a one-bedroom apartment and eating chicken noodle soup because they've spent all their money on one last-ditch effort to find a rich spouse and they both picked the wrong pauper."

"You really think she's not rich?" Virgie eyed the woman.

"No, she's not rich. And she's only about seventy. She wants to look old enough to make a man think she's got one foot in the grave and the other on a pod of boiled okra. The man then thinks he's only got to endure the marriage until she dies and he gets all the money. She won't even ask for a prenup. She'll tell him she's so much in love with him it doesn't matter about their assets. That makes him feels guilty if he asks for one. Then she uses him up and buries him and gets all those glorious dollars. This time Luella or whatever name she's going by now will get a good dose of her own medicine. After all, she thinks he's rich. He thinks she is. They'll both have a rude awakening when it comes time for the honeymoon and neither of them has a dime," Hannah said.

"You sure?"

"Yep, I'm positive. She worked the Brewer Hotel about five years ago. Thought I recognized her when Buford first honed in on her. She's from around DC, I think. Married a man from Morgantown and made him move to New York. He died about a year ago. Guess his money is gone."

"What do you mean, worked the hotel?" Virgie asked.

"Checked in for a week. Paid up front with cash and made sure she and her glittery fake jewels were visible every waking moment. Spent lots of time in the lobby and lingered over dinner every evening. It worked really well."

"Think I should warn Buford?" Myrtle asked.

"Be a waste of time and breath. He's on the prowl for a rich woman. She's hunting a rich man. It will be poetic justice, and he wouldn't believe you anyway," Hannah answered.

"I like the picture of them eating chicken noodle soup," Virgie said.

"You're right. Those diamonds are too damn big to be real. If they were honest-to-God diamonds, someone would have already knocked her in the head and stolen them." Virgie squinted at the woman, who smiled and patted Buford's hand.

"Well, I haven't found a single man on this ship I'd take home," Edith said.

"Guess we've gotten old and picky," Myrtle said.

"No, they've gotten old and silly," Hannah told them.

"Amen." They raised their glasses in unison.

"To our friendship." Hannah raised hers to touch theirs. "May it endure this life and follow us to the other side."

"Does that scare you?" Edith asked when they'd downed the contents of their wineglasses and set them back on the table.

"What?"

"The other side?"

"Used to. Then I read this quote and figured it was true. Haven't been scared since. Figure it'll happen and God will do just what he promised," Hannah said.

"What's the quote?"

"It says, 'When we come to the edge of the light we know and are about to step off into the darkness of the unknown, of this we can be sure...either God will provide something solid to stand on or we will be taught to fly.' I can't remember who said it or even if I ever knew, but a few months ago when the doctor said I needed that surgery and I'd just as soon gone on and died, it was comforting," Hannah said.

"I like it. I hope I get the wings," Edith said.

"I'm not so sure heaven would be safe if we all four got wings," Hannah said.

❖ ❖ ❖

Karen wiped sweat from her brow as she went into the house through the garage door. They'd thought southern Oklahoma was the devil's playground back in the early part of June. At the end of August, they found out June had been the pleasant time of summer. The thermometer had registered at least a hundred and five degrees every day for the whole month.

She filled a glass with ice and sweet tea and sat down at the dining room table to study the jam labels the designers had come up with. Still staring at the labels, she heard weeping in the living room. She pushed the chair back and found no one in the room and the sobs coming from the office. When she peeped in the door, Kim had her head on the desk in front of the computer monitor. Her shoulders were heaving with every sob.

Karen touched her shoulder. "Kim, what is it?"

Kim jumped as if she'd been shot, and wiped at her eyes. "I'm being silly. I miss Nanna."

"Well, honey, she'll be home in four days. They'll arrive in New York tomorrow and then on into Dallas after that. You've gone longer than two weeks without seeing her before now." Karen rubbed her neck.

"But that was in Morgantown. That was when she was a prissy old woman who dressed up and went to dinner every evening. Now she's a real person who gets her hands dirty in the garden and cusses and makes me laugh. And I miss her. I like her calls every night to tell us all the funny things that are happening, but I miss her being right here." Fresh sobs erupted as Kim pushed the chair back, stood up, and threw her arms around Karen.

"Me too, honey. Who would have thought we'd be so homesick to see her," Karen said.

"I guess it's because I'm pregnant," Kim said as she wiped her eyes. "I'm all weepy and hungry and I'm getting too fat for my clothes and I don't know what to do about marrying Luke. I love him, but the first year of marriage is supposed to be all wonderful, not pregnant and fat and ugly. And I'm worried about liking John so much. Is that disrespectful to my daddy's memory?"

"Darlin' girl, this is all hormonal. I promise you'll feel better in a day or two. Your father was a wonderful man. He would have wanted your mother to be happy, and you should not feel guilty. Come on and sit with me in the dining room. I've got an important decision to make. It'll take your mind off all your worries. Let's go have some lemonade and we'll talk," Karen said.

"But what about me and Luke? You didn't tell me to marry him or to wait." Kim filled two glasses with ice.

"That's something you have to decide. If you love him and can't bear to be without him, then marry him. If you have a doubt, wait. Do you realize how many conversations we've had this summer sitting around this table or working in the kitchen?"

Kim sniffed, pulled two paper towels from the spool, and blew her nose loudly. "I don't think I'm going to let her go again. This all started when I thought of her this morning. Do you ever think about going back to Morgantown? Do you ever miss your friends there?"

"No and no. I can't believe I ever lived anywhere else. No, I wouldn't go back, and no, I don't miss my friends. Nowadays, I tell you and Sue and Mother everything, and I like my life. I like where it's going. I'm sorry Norma had to die, but I'm glad she left the farm to Mother because it's changed all of our lives for the better. How about you? Do you miss your little friends?"

Tears filled her eyes again. "I did those first couple of days, but then we were so busy with everything and Luke was here and he was so good-looking and nice to me, and it's almost like God took Norma at the right time to bring us all four together, isn't it? That sounds so selfish and cruel."

"Maybe, but I really think that she knew what she wanted but she couldn't get it during this life, so she fixed things so they'd happen after she was gone. Let's get our mind off your nanna and you can help me make a difficult decision," Karen said, changing the subject.

"What?"

"The designer has come up with two labels for my new food stuff. One that he thought I'd like and…"

"Ohhhh," Kim picked up the one Karen had already rejected. "Ugly, isn't it?"

"No, it's great. It's kind of old-fashioned looking with the vines all tangled around the outside of the words. You'll do great with this label."

Karen cocked her head to the side and picked up the paper.

Kim said, "I like the name, Emet's Best. You'll be giving those big names some competition."

"I'll just be satisfied to turn the garage into a little specialty shop this year," Karen said.

"It's going to be the next big thing. Just wait and see. But you need to change the label color with each jam. Hot pink for strawberry. Lime green for your new pepper jelly and a darker green for the mint. And then deep blue for the blackberry and grape."

"I agree. I can see it in hot pink and I like it even better than this brown one." Karen nodded.

"Now, I can't wait for Nanna to get home for sure. She's going to love this label." Kim picked it up and drew an imaginary watermelon vine with her fingertips. "I can already see it all made up and on the shelf ready to buy."

"But can you see some old cowboy in boots and a buckle bigger than his ego coming into my shop to buy it for his girlfriend's birthday?"

"Sure. And he'll order it all made up in a gift basket and put the key to a fancy hotel room on the ribbon," Kim teased.

Karen's eyes widened. "You need to go into advertising. I can see a thirty-second television commercial with a handsome

Texan and the gleam in his eyes as the woman all decked out in diamonds picks it up and leads him up a winding stairway carpeted in pink. The slogan will be 'Taste Emet's Best and get a taste of heaven.'"

"We'll do it. We'll get in touch with a television company. Surely one of the new and rising stars will endorse our new line."

"And it'll promote six million in sales!"

"Look at us," Kim said. "Would we have done this in Morgantown? A new, spunky label and talking about sexy television commercials?"

Karen shook her head. "Mother is going to be so excited and we'll have news for her after she tells us all about her trip. Can you believe the garden is going to be ready when she gets here? I can't wait to show it to her all finished. Do you think we need to blindfold her?"

"Oh, yeah, and make a big deal out of the whole thing. Hey we need to have a memorial service with us and the ladies and John and Luke and..." Kim's eyes glittered as she planned more than just saying a few words out of the Bible for Norma.

CHAPTER TWENTY-ONE

The pink memorial stone at the head of the garden was etched with gold lettering. On either side water flowed over natural stones Luke and John had gathered from the fields. Koi swam where the miniature falls cascaded into pools surrounded by greenery and plants. At frequent intervals, the sprinkler system was set automatically to alternately water or mist to keep everything tropical green. One verdigris wrought-iron bench faced the stone; two others flanked it with a matching coffee table in the middle. A pathway of stepping-stones went from the gate beside the patio to the benches. Grass as thick and lush as carpet covered the ground inside the fenced area. Asters, mums, petunias, roses, marigolds, rose moss, and lantana looked as if they'd been growing there for years instead of weeks.

At six o'clock on that Friday evening, a small parade of people opened the gate. Hannah, dressed in a blue pantsuit, with her hair done up in a French roll, makeup applied, fingernails polished, and diamonds glittering in the evening sun, led the procession. Karen, dressed in a forest-green sheath dress with a jacket in a lighter shade, looped her arm in Edith's and they took their place behind the middle bench.

Sue had barely had time to shower and change from a day out on the tractor, getting the last cutting of hay for the year. She wore a flowing orange skirt that barely touched her ankles, a matching cotton sweater with an Aztec sun spraying across the front, and soft tawny-colored sandals. John's jeans were starched and creased, his boots shined brightly, and his pale yellow shirt was unbuttoned at the neck. They stood behind the bench on the north side.

Luke wore a western-cut suit complete with a white shirt and vest. His shirt was unbuttoned at the neck. Kim had chosen a pale blue dress with more than twenty white pearl buttons up the front. Her engagement ring sparkled against the setting sun. She held hands with Luke all the way down the stepping-stone path and stood behind the southern bench.

After that, Myrtle and Virgie took their places, sitting in front of Sue and John. Myrtle wore an outfit she'd bought in Hamilton, Bermuda. A lovely pink linen with a darker shade of roses embroidered around the slim skirt and jacket. Virgie wore a red ruffled dress of georgette and an enormous black hat with red silk roses on one side.

The preacher waited at the front until they were all seated.

"We'll have a minute of silence," Hannah said.

Everyone bowed their heads, shut their eyes, and waited.

Hannah broke the silence after a moment. "Norma, we have come to scatter your ashes in this garden. You always said you didn't want to spend eternity in a six-foot hole, so I've made a place for you that you'll love. It seems only right that they are here, since this is where I intend to come to visit with you. I miss you, my friend. Happy birthday." She picked up the wooden box sitting beside her and carefully poured the ashes on the grass in front of the stone, which simply had Norma's name, dates of her birth and death, and a quotation: *Strolling Over Heaven*. The girls would find, when they opened the letter the hour after she died, that there was room for her name on the stone and her ashes were to be put in the same place. Two old friends together forever in the rich Oklahoma dirt.

When she finished, she wiped her eyes with a lace-trimmed handkerchief she pulled from her pocket and sat back down.

The preacher moved to the side of the stone. "We are gathered here today in the presence of God and these faithful friends to remember Norma Andrews. Proverbs 18:24 says, 'There is a friend that sticketh closer than a brother.' Norma was that to lots of people. Some are sitting here today. She didn't have a natural brother or sister, but she was both blessed and a blessing."

It was perfect. Prettier than Hannah had imagined it could be. It had taken a lot of work, but it had all come together in time for Norma's birthday, and that's what Hannah wanted: to be able to open the garden on that very day.

Kim cleared her throat and moved to stand beside the stone. "This isn't in the plans, Nanna, and I hope it doesn't ruin your day, but Luke and I've been doing some serious talking and thinking. If we could have what we want, we would have Norma right here in the flesh with us, but that's not possible. However, before the rain and wind takes even the last of her ashes from us, we'd like to at least have that much today. We've decided to marry this evening in this garden if no one has any objections."

"What a lovely birthday present," Edith said.

Luke joined Kim and took her hand in his. "We bought a license the first of the week and the preacher is here. So is that all right with you, Hannah?"

"I can't think of a better gift to give Norma." Hannah wiped at her eyes, smearing mascara all over the white handkerchief.

"Mother?" Kim asked. After all, she was the only daughter, the only child.

"It's a wonderful idea." Sue's chin quivered.

"Well, then…" The preacher smiled. "I don't have my book, but I think I can remember enough to get the job done.

"Dearly beloved, we are gathered here before God and these witnesses, both physical and spiritual, to join this man and woman together in holy matrimony. If anyone has a reason they should not marry, let them speak now or forever hold their peace." He waited ten seconds before he went on.

In fifteen minutes, the ceremony was finished. A gust of early fall wind stirred the ashes in front of the memorial stone, sending them swirling about. Hannah watched as the breeze picked up and carried some of them straight up to the clouds.

"It's Friday night, so we planned supper, but we don't have a wedding cake or anything for a bride and groom." Sue hugged her daughter as soon as the long, lingering wedding kiss was finished.

John had given her a lovely engagement ring for her birthday, and they were thinking about a December wedding. Maybe in one of the islands. Nothing fancy. Just the two of them on a beach somewhere with a preacher.

"It's exactly what we wanted," Kim said. "I moved all my things from the bedroom over to our house today."

"So I finally get my own room," Karen teased.

John led the way out of the garden and into the house. "Steaks, potatoes on the grill, corn on the cob, and one of Sue's famous peach cobblers are waiting. Fifteen minutes and we'll have the table set."

"I'm on my way," Edith said.

Hannah listened to the excited chatter as she joined her friends to walk from the garden, but she didn't hear the words. She remembered another wedding on this property, as informal as this one. It hadn't been a bad life with Jesse. Far from it. By the time he died, they'd been good friends, but she had always wanted so much more for her girls. It had taken coming here to find it, and Hannah didn't regret leaving that other life behind one bit.

Karen remembered her own wedding: the finest affair in Morgantown. The biggest church looked like someone had sprayed it down with lavender silk and rounded up all the purple flowers in the state for the ten bridesmaids' bouquets, and to decorate the church and the country club reception hall. The ice sculpture was six feet tall, carved to look like wedding bells, and the honeymoon was in Italy. All those thousands of dollars and even in those first days, Daniel hadn't looked at her like Luke did Kim.

When they'd finished eating, Kim sat down beside Karen and hugged her.

"There weren't any doubts," she whispered in her grandmother's ear.

"I can see that. What did you do about Marshall Neville?" Karen asked.

"I called Nanna's lawyer. Then I called Marshall. I told him I was pregnant and the line went dead silent. He said he'd try to send me the money to take care of it and I told him I was not going to have an abortion. He was really messed up until I made him be quiet and let me talk. The gist of what I said is that I don't want a dime. He said he should take care of his responsibility. I assured him I didn't want money but

I wanted him to sign away parental rights. That way when they're born they'll be Luke's."

"Did he?"

"He wasn't sure he felt right about it, but he sure didn't want Amelia to know. I reminded him he had a choice. Sign the papers, which the lawyer would be bringing to him, or pay me child support on twins, and there was no way he could keep that from Amelia. He mumbled something about me proving he was the father and DNA tests. I agreed. He's a good man, Grandma. It had to be difficult for him. The papers are signed, sealed, and in my file cabinet. These twins belong to Luke. Ask anyone in town." Kim smiled.

"You did the right thing," Karen said.

Luke carried Kim over the threshold into his house later that evening. He set her down long enough to push a button on the CD player. Mark Chesnutt's voice came through the speakers, singing "Old Country." It told a tale of a country boy and a city girl, how he'd just plowed until noon and how she'd never been loved at all until old country came to town. It wasn't a romantic wedding song, but Kim knew exactly what Luke was saying as he two-stepped with her all over the living room.

"It says they get together every now and then," he whispered. "But this old country boy is going to spend the rest of his life with you."

"This city girl is going to enjoy every minute of it." She laid her head on his chest and listened to the song as it played a second time.

"Country boys don't get in a hurry, you know." He kissed her ear.

"About what?"

"Anything."

"Sounds like an exciting ride through life," she told him.

He scooped her up and carried her to the bedroom where candles were lit. "Regretting not having a honeymoon?"

"No regrets. When I get where I'm going there'll be no secrets. That's what Nanna said once. I love you, Luke. Besides, this is our honeymoon, and I expect it to last for at least seventy years."

He laid her gently on the bed and very slowly began to unfasten the two dozen buttons down the front of her pale blue dress.

❖ ❖ ❖

"It's strange, her being gone," Sue said that evening as the three of them sat in the living room, sipping lemonade.

"She's not gone. She's just not right here. We'll see her every day," Karen said. "At least beginning Monday. I don't expect to see much of them before then. But Luke will have school and she'll be back in the office doing our accounting work."

"Think Norma is happy?" Sue asked.

"I think this is a bonus," Hannah said. "What Norma wanted most was for you and John to get together. When you get married the clouds will part, I'm sure."

"Do you ever want to go back and redo it all? Turn back the clock and not come out here?" Sue asked Hannah.

"Not a single minute. I'm more alive than I've ever been. This is the best time of my whole life. I wouldn't change a single minute of it and I hope there's lots more harvests and cruises in store before I really do stroll over heaven with Norma."

Karen raised her glass. "Me too. I was alive in Morgantown, but I'm living here. It's the most wonderful feeling in the world."

"You think you'll ever find someone?" Sue asked.

"Not for a minute," she mimicked Hannah. "I'm not ever marrying again. How about you, Sue? I had this same conversation with Kim a few weeks ago. She couldn't decide whether to marry Luke now or wait until the babies were born. I told her if she had doubts to wait. She assured me tonight there were no doubts. Are you going to have regrets someday? You're the one giving up a teaching job and more friends than any of us had in Morgantown, plus you still had Jeff's family out there."

"No regrets," Sue said. "None whatsoever. In Morgantown, I felt guilty every time I looked at another man. Jeff's mother and sisters and his brother were always there in the back of my mind, telling me that I would be disrespecting his memory. Then there was the guilt from Corky. I'm so glad Kim doesn't have the baggage we all had."

"Amen." Karen raised her glass again.

EPILOGUE

One year later

Hannah donned a denim jacket that morning. A norther
had whipped down from Kansas the night before, drop-
ping the temperature twenty degrees in five minutes. A
bit unusual for September, but Oklahoma never promised
steady, predictable weather. Tomorrow it might be back up
to a hundred degrees.

She poured a cup of decaffeinated coffee. She hated the
taste, but the doctor had given her a good report on her last
visit. Her cholesterol was down and her heart sounded good.
Carrying the coffee with her, she went to the garden. She sat
down on the middle bench and envisioned Norma sitting on
the grass in front of the memorial stone. In her imagination,
Norma always wore the same overalls she'd worn in the picture still sitting on the dresser.

Hannah held up the cup in a toast.

"Happy birthday, my friend. We are now both eighty-one
years old. It's been a good year, full of surprises," she said in
a conversational tone, just as if Norma were sitting in front
of the stone.

"We buried Myrtle last week, but you probably knew about that before we did. We had coffee that morning and she talked about remodeling her bathroom. Said she needed one of those step-in showers because it was getting to be too much for her hip to get in and out of the bathtub. Thought she just might fix the whole thing for wheelchair-bound folks since there could come a time when she would have to depend on one. Said that she hoped she never was confined to such a thing and that night she just fell asleep and woke up on the other side with her set of wings. She got her wish that very night. I hope you had a long talk with God and she had something solid to stand on or else you taught her to fly. I miss her, Norma, but I bet you two are sure having a good time.

"We had a wonderful cruise this year. Our crops were better than they were last year and I'm already looking forward to next year's harvest. Anyway, I was telling you about the cruise. We went to the Bahamas. Stayed ten days. It was wonderful.

"Now down to the family business. As you know, Luke and Kim's kids are seven months old now. Norma Jane and Hannah Rose, but to us they are Janey and Rosy. You know all that, though. The big surprise is the miracle. Remember, Luke wasn't supposed to be able to make any babies. Well, he did, and it looks like we get twins again this time around. Rosy and Janey will be fourteen months old when they are born. Ain't that a hoot? We're turning the place into a baby ranch! Doctor says these two are boys.

"The living room looks like a day care center with swings, playpens, and all the things to help me take care of the babies while Kim does the book work, which seems to get bigger and bigger. Karen talked Sue into putting more garden into strawberries and starting another grape arbor for her jam business. She's made the garage into a cute little shop, and there's a constant flow of traffic in and out of here, buying jams and produce. You should see the commercial she's got on television. The actor is so sexy it would make your heart do double time. Kim calls him eye candy. And Tillman called this last week and asked Karen to go to dinner and she actually said yes.

"Another surprise happened this year too. Sue and John got married and settled into his place last November. She thought she was old at forty, but she found out that she was just getting started. She got pregnant on the honeymoon. Guess it was Jeff's fault they never had kids past Kim. I don't think I've ever heard Kim laugh so hard in her life. She said before it was over we would have an 'I'm my own grandpa' situation. The baby was a boy, and they named him Ricky after your Ricky.

"I'm not slowing down a bit. Somehow, you did just the right thing when you brought us all together. I expect I'm trying to make up for the lean years and cram as much as I can into these last ones. They're full and I'm happy. What more could an old lady ask out of life?

"I hear the van coming down the lane. Kim's on her way with the children and Sue will be here soon with Ricky. Edith and Virgie will show up sometime this morning for coffee and to play with the babies. Life is good, Norma. I'll be back to visit again soon. Have a good time with Myrtle. She'll fill you in on the rest of the gossip. What's that?" Hannah cocked her head to one side, straining to hear the whisper of a voice floating in the fall breeze. Of course, she couldn't actually hear Norma talking to her but she could well imagine what she would be saying if she could speak that morning.

Finally, Hannah nodded. "You know I will. They're yours as much as mine."

Hannah was coming in the back door when Kim carried the first child through the garage and kitchen. "Nanna, where are you?"

"Right here, child. Been out talking to Norma. She sends her love."

ACKNOWLEDGMENTS

Dear Reader,

Welcome to Emet, Oklahoma, a tiny little town just south of Milburn. The post office is gone and the kids are bussed into Milburn these days, since there's no school in Emet, but the people there are friendly and the community is still strong.

When I went looking for a place to set *Hidden Secrets*, Husband and I drove down through Tishomingo and then on to Milburn, but nothing reached out and grabbed my attention until we got to Emet. I knew when we rounded that last curve into town that I'd found the right place for Hannah and her girls. It had the feel that I wanted, and I could visualize the farm with Luke's ranch on one side and John's on the other. And then I saw the perfect place for the fruit stand.

Secrets had been hiding in Hannah, Karen, Sue, and Kim's past but in Emet, where they have to live together in a small house and work together in the garden, the orchard, and the fruit stand, they find more than a bloodline connecting them as the secrets come out one by one and reshape their lives and futures.

Thanks to Montlake Publishing, to Kelli Martin, and to Folio Literary Management for making this book a reality.

Thanks to all my readers who continue to support me by reading my books, telling their neighbors over the backyard fence about my books, and sharing my books with their friends. Big thanks to Husband, who continues to support me and drive all over southern Oklahoma and Texas while I take notes for new books. It takes a special person to be married to an author, and I appreciate all that he does to make my job easier.

Happy Reading,
Carolyn Brown

ABOUT THE AUTHOR

Carolyn L. Brown is the author of the *New York Times* and *USA Today* bestselling novel *Love Drunk Cowboy*, as well as *I Love This Bar, One Hot Cowboy Wedding*, RITA finalist *The Ladies' Room*, and several other sassy romances. Born in Texas and raised in southern Oklahoma, she has three grown children and enough grandchildren to keep her young. She lives with her husband in Oklahoma.